Dear Diary,

My life is out of control! According to the provision in our kooky fathers' wills, Blake and I have to marry and produce an heir within a year. Otherwise, we'll never be able to claim our rightful inheritance. Blake can be ruthless in business and so calm and composed, it's downright disturbing! But there are moments when I glimpse a different man. Sure he's cold and aloof on the surface, but his warm, passionate side manages to catch me off guard. And there is something about him that I find quite disarming. Not that I'd ever admit it to his face. And what a face he has.... He's the most devastatingly handsome man I've ever known.

But each day as my belly grows bigger with our unborn child, I worry about what kind of family life we'll be able to give him or her. I want so much to provide our baby with a warm, loving environment, but can Blake and I bond as husband and wife? I have no idea how all of this will work out, but I do know that this little one inside me means everything to me. And I'm beginning to feel the same way about Blake....

FAMILY

1. **HOUSEBOUND—** *Anne Stuart*
2. **MOONLIGHT AND LACE—** *Linda Turner*
3. **MOTHER KNOWS BEST—** *Barbara Bretton*
4. **THE BABY BARGAIN—** *Dallas Schulze*
5. **A FINE ARRANGEMENT—** *Helen R. Myers*
6. **WHERE THERE'S A WILL—** *Day Leclaire*
7. **BEYOND SUMMER—** *Karen Young*
8. **MOTHER FOR HIRE—** *Marie Ferrarella*
9. **OBSESSION—** *Lisa Jackson*
10. **TRUST A HERO—** *Muriel Jensen*
11. **GAUNTLET RUN—** *Joan Elliott Pickart*
12. **WEDNESDAY'S CHILD—** *Leigh Michaels*
13. **FREE SPIRITS—** *Linda Randall Wisdom*
14. **CUPID CONNECTION—** *Leandra Logan*
15. **SLOW LARKIN'S REVENGE—** *Christine Rimmer*
16. **UNHEAVENLY ANGEL—** *Annette Broadrick*
17. **THE LIGHTS OF HOME—** *Marilyn Pappano*
18. **JOEY'S FATHER—** *Elizabeth August*
19. **CHANGE OF LIFE—** *Judith Arnold*
20. **BOUND FOR BLISS—** *Kristine Rolofson*
21. **IN FROM THE RAIN—** *Gina Wilkins*
22. **LOVE ME AGAIN—** *Ann Major*
23. **ON THE WHISPERING WIND—** *Nikki Benjamin*
24. **A PERFECT PAIR—** *Karen Toller Whittenburg*
25. **THE MARINER'S BRIDE—** *Bronwyn Williams*
26. **NO WALLS BETWEEN US—** *Naomi Horton*
27. **STRINGS—** *Muriel Jensen*
28. **BLINDMAN'S BLUFF—** *Lass Small*
29. **ANOTHER CHANCE AT HEAVEN—** *Elda Minger*
30. **JOURNEY'S END—** *Bobby Hutchinson*
31. **TANGLED WEB—** *Cathy Gillen Thacker*
32. **DOUBLE TROUBLE—** *Barbara Boswell*
33. **GOOD TIME MAN—** *Emilie Richards*
34. **DONE TO PERFECTION—** *Stella Bagwell*
35. **POWDER RIVER REUNION—** *Myrna Temte*
36. **A CORNER OF HEAVEN—** *Theresa Michaels*
37. **TOGETHER AGAIN—** *Ruth Jean Dale*
38. **PRINCE OF DELIGHTS—** *Renee Roszel*
39. **'TIL THERE WAS YOU—** *Kathleen Eagle*
40. **OUT ON A LIMB—** *Victoria Pade*
41. **SHILOH'S PROMISE—** *BJ James*
42. **A SEASON FOR HOMECOMING—** *Laurie Paige*
43. **THE FLAMING—** *Pat Tracy*
44. **DREAM CHASERS—** *Anne McAllister*
45. **ALL THAT GLITTERS—** *Kristine Rolofson*
46. **SUGAR HILL—** *Beverly Barton*
47. **FANTASY MAN—** *Paula Detmer Riggs*
48. **KEEPING CHRISTMAS—** *Marisa Carroll*
49. **JUST LIKE OLD TIMES—** *Jennifer Greene*
50. **A WARRIOR'S HEART—** *Margaret Moore*

FAMILY

Annette BROADRICK

Unheavenly Angel

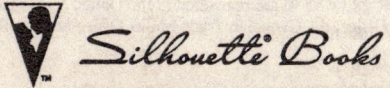

Published by Silhouette Books

America's Publisher of Contemporary Romance

If you purchased this book without a cover you should be aware that this book is stolen property. It was reported as "unsold and destroyed" to the publisher, and neither the author nor the publisher has received any payment for this "stripped book."

 SILHOUETTE BOOKS
300 East 42nd St.,
New York, N.Y. 10017

ISBN 0-373-82164-6

UNHEAVENLY ANGEL

Copyright © 1986 by Annette Broadrick

All rights reserved. Except for use in any review, the reproduction or utilization of this work in whole or in part in any form by any electronic, mechanical or other means, now known or hereafter invented, including xerography, photocopying and recording, or in any information storage or retrieval system, is forbidden without the written permission of the editorial office, Silhouette Books, 300 East 42nd Street, New York, NY 10017 U.S.A.

All characters in this book have no existence outside the imagination of the author and have no relation whatsoever to anyone bearing the same name or names. They are not even distantly inspired by any individual known or unknown to the author, and all incidents are pure invention.

This edition published by arrangement with Harlequin Books S.A.

® and TM are trademarks of Harlequin Books S.A., used under license. Trademarks indicated with ® are registered in the United States Patent and Trademark Office, the Canadian Trade Marks Office and in other countries.

Visit us at www.romance.net

Printed in U.S.A.

Dear Reader,

I'm delighted that this story is being brought out with the FAMILY reissue program because it is one of my favorites.

I had an idea to put two people together who were opposites in every way and force them to find a central ground on which to build a life. It was easy to come up with Angel—a free spirit who enjoys creating—because I could draw on my own background and attitudes toward life.

It was more difficult to come up with Blake, her opposite, a man who was so wrapped up in his job that he has little time for anyone else. While I was discussing my idea with a family member, she laughingly suggested that I had just described my son, Rick, who was very dedicated to his profession.

So throughout the story, whenever I needed Blake to move the action along, I would ask myself, "What would Rick do in this situation?" and I'd immediately have my next scene.

Of course I told him that he was the model for my hero and he was quite pleased...until he read the book. "Mom, surely I'm not *that* unromantic," he complained. The love of his life and I looked at each other and laughed.

Like Blake, Rick has learned that there's more to life than his career—such as his daughter, Phelan.

This is a fun story. I hope you enjoy it.

Annette Broadrick

Please address questions and book requests to:
Silhouette Reader Service
U.S.: 3010 Walden Ave., P.O. Box 1325, Buffalo, NY 14269
Canadian: P.O. Box 609, Fort Erie, Ont. L2A 5X3

This novel is dedicated to the memory of my father,
Wilford Allen Hensley.

Chapter One

Harrison Tyler wearily rubbed his forehead. For the first time in his fifty-five years, he felt old. Harry sat behind the impressive desk that served as the focal point of Scott Bennington's large and well-stocked library. Never before had he occupied the seat behind the desk because Scott had always been there. Until now.

Harry studied the two young people seated across from him and once again was reminded of his age. How had time slipped away from him? He clearly remembered the day Blake Carlyle was born. How could he possibly forget the three of them—he, Todd Carlyle and Scott Bennington celebrating the arrival of Todd's firstborn by getting rip-roaring drunk.

That had been more than thirty-two years ago.

Thirty-two years. What had happened to all those years? There were still so many things the three men, friends since grade school, had intended to do together. Not that they hadn't done a hell of a lot in their lifetimes. But for some reason they had behaved as though they would live forever—as though nothing could possibly harm them.

Scott and Todd had been wrong.

Now it was left to Harry to inform their offspring of the plans Scott and Todd had made for their children. He wasn't looking forward to the telling.

His gaze fell admiringly on Angel Bennington. Angel had been a beauty since the day she was born, almost twenty-six years ago, which was why Scott—in an uncharacteristic outburst of sentimentality—had insisted on naming her Angel.

She had always been tiny for her age, reminding Harry of a sprite flitting among the massive furniture amassed by generations of Benningtons, looking almost as out of place as her mother had obviously felt. Angel had been only five when Yvette had declared, in her lightly accented tone, that she would never be happy living in San Francisco, despite all of Scott's inducements and promises, and that she and, of course, *la belle* Angel were returning to the civilized world, which to Yvette, of course, could only mean France.

Scott had been devastated, but he had survived. When Angel was older he convinced Yvette to allow

Angel to visit San Francisco each summer, and he flew to France several times a year to see her.

The adult Angel still looked like a pixie sitting there before him. A very sad pixie. She had lost the father she adored, just as Harry had lost his two closest friends.

No one knew what Blake was feeling. No one ever did.

When Scott and Todd decided to go into the electronics business several years before, microchips had rarely been heard of and their function only vaguely guessed at. Harry had been their attorney and had watched the business mushroom into a multimillion-dollar corporation—privately owned. All of the stock had been held by the two men, although they had offered Harry shares when they first started. He sometimes wondered if things might have turned out differently if he'd agreed to take the shares. But he hadn't.

Scott and Todd took turns being chairman of the board and president of the company, alternating each year. They almost made a game of it.

Blake had gone to work for the company as soon as he graduated from Harvard. No doubt he was aware he was being groomed to take over the business someday, some mythical, far-off day when Todd and Scott no longer cared to work or preferred to explore the world. What nobody had expected was a plane crash in the Orient, killing all passengers, including fifty-five-year-old Todd Carlyle and fifty-four-year-old Scott Bennington.

Of course they had made provisions for their offspring in the unlikely event something unforeseen happened to them. Unfortunately they treated the whole thing as a joke. The idea they hatched between them was the result of an all-night poker party that had been liberally endowed with a great deal of booze. Harry couldn't remember which one of them first suggested the outrageous idea because they both immediately roared with laughter and decided that the suggestion merited considerable thought.

Harry had felt certain that by dawn's sober light they would forget it. Unfortunately they hadn't. He spent weeks trying to talk them out of their plan but they were having none of his arguments. It was only when they threatened to find another attorney to draw up the papers, because, after all, what they were proposing was in no way illegal (outrageous, perhaps, but certainly not illegal), that Harry agreed to draw up the buy-sell agreement—a routine document in a partnership—as well as a will for each of them.

Perhaps things might have been different if Blake's mother had not died when he was ten. Lydia Blake Carlyle had always been a cool, aloof woman. Henry had never understood how the warmhearted, fun-loving Todd Carlyle had ever fallen for such a cold, seemingly unfeeling woman. But perhaps she could have exerted some influence over the proceedings and made the men face the impropriety of what they were suggesting. He certainly hadn't been able to do so.

Studying the man seated before him, Harry found himself secretly wondering if Todd's only son had had the misfortune of taking after his mother.

Blake wasn't cold, exactly. Reserved was a better description of his personality. He had his father's height and muscular build and his mother's dark coloring, but it was his roguish smile, so seldom witnessed by those not close to him, that reminded Harry that Blake was very much Todd's son.

Blake had had little to smile about, however, during these past several days. It had fallen on him to arrange the double funeral, to contact Angel in France and arrange for her arrival in San Francisco to coincide with the services, and to continue running the business that Scott and Todd had left.

It was the disposition of the business that was the crux of the matter now.

Harry cleared his throat, pointedly looking first at Blake, then at Angel. Blake's compelling black-eyed stare steadily met his, while Angel's large, sapphire-blue gaze caused a lump to form in Harry's throat. The fiery flame of her burnished curls gave an aureole effect to her countenance. With her sad expression she did, indeed, appear to be a grieving angel.

"I'm sure you two understand how very difficult

all of this has been for me," he began, studying his folded hands lying on the desk in front of him. "As you both are aware, my friendship with your fathers spans almost fifty years. And since I never married, you two are the closest I have ever come to having children. I have watched both of you grow and mature...."

He paused because he detected a faint trickle of moisture fall from Angel's left eye and realized that at the rate he was going, he would have all three of them sobbing very shortly.

"I don't believe that Scott or Todd ever imagined that the documents I am about to read to you would ever be put into effect. I am ashamed to say that I feel they were meant to be an attempt at their brand of rather ribald humor. Had either of you married before their deaths, I am sure changes would have been made immediately."

Blake Carlyle shifted in his chair, startled at the mention of marriage. He couldn't imagine what their being married would have to do with the disposition of the estates. Surely the situation was simple enough, since he and Angel were the only ones in line to inherit.

Blake had been eleven years old when Yvette Bennington and Angel had moved to France. He remembered Angel's mother very well. She had been vivacious, outgoing and very striking with her splash of red hair, ivory skin and lustrous green eyes.

Blake's mother had despised her. Had she lived, Lydia Carlyle would have been the first to point out that she had predicted the marriage would not last. She would have been right. As far back as Blake could remember, his mother had always been right. She had even predicted her own rather untimely death. Almost no one died of pneumonia anymore, not since the advent of penicillin. But Lydia Carlyle did. Blake had sometimes wondered if she might actually have died in order to prove that she had been right and everyone else had been wrong.

But her opinions of the woman who had produced and directed the upbringing of the young woman seated beside him had colored his opinion of both.

Blake looked at Angel impassively. He found even her name distasteful. Nobody was named Angel, except perhaps a burlesque queen. Although he recognized that she could not be held responsible for the name she had been given at birth, she had made no effort to change it, although Angelique didn't sound much better to him. It brought to mind some bawdy French madam.

His gaze returned to Harrison Tyler. Never had he seen Harry quite so agitated, almost unstrung, although it wasn't particularly surprising. After all, he had just said goodbye to his two closest friends. Blake himself still couldn't believe the men weren't going to come through that door momentarily, admitting it had all been some macabre joke, laughing that the rest of them had fallen for it.

He knew his life would never be the same without them.

Angel was valiantly struggling not to cry in front of the two men. Not that she really minded crying in front of Harry, who had bounced her on his knee as far back as she could remember. He and Todd had often accompanied her father on his visit to France and she had always considered them as part of her family. She knew that Harry could understand her grief at the abrupt cessation of the loving relationship she had shared with her father. Angel had loved her father with a fierce, undying loyalty that nothing or no one could sway. Her mother had found her energetic defense of her oftentimes absent father rather exhausting and totally boring and had allowed her only child—and she had made it clear to all who would listen how thankful she was to have had only one child—to hero-worship to her heart's content.

Now he was gone.

Angel surreptitiously wiped a tear away. She did not want to show her grief in front of Blake Carlyle. She barely knew the man. They had seen each other very infrequently during the years Angel had traveled back and forth between France and the United States.

Although six years older, Blake had always seemed to be an adult to her. Perhaps it was because he was so serious and reserved. She had never known what to say to him and had avoided him as much as possible.

Blake appeared to be nothing at all like his father, who had been a warm and affectionate person, full of fun and with a sense of adventure the young Angel had appreciated. She could see none of that in his son. He seemed to be at home in the business world, a world so foreign to Angel it could have been on another planet.

According to her father, Blake had a natural flair for the business and an unusual ability to identify the underlying problems in a given situation and be able to provide a workable solution. Her father had greatly admired Blake, and Angel trusted her father's judgment implicitly.

She was the first to acknowledge, however, she and Blake had absolutely nothing in common.

Her thoughts, emotions and ambitions centered on the art world. The young, lonely child had gravitated toward the solitary occupation of art, finding solace in the bright colors and the expression of her emotions on canvas. Thus she poured all of her passionate feelings into her paintings, spending her youth taking lessons and attending classes in Paris.

Her first painting sold when she was sixteen. Her mother was killed in a car crash in southern France when Angel was nineteen. By the time she was twenty-one Angel was living in Paris in an apartment building filled with painters, sculptors and students of art. She didn't need to worry about money because of the income derived from the trust Scott had set up for her when she was born. Additionally, during the ten years she had been painting professionally her work had increased in value and her style and technique were beginning to be recognized throughout the art world.

No one, now that her father was gone, knew how successful Angel had become with her painting. It had been a joke between them that the halo she used as her signature on each of her paintings had been interpreted to mean a ring or a gold band of some sort. Those who insisted on knowing the artist's name were given the name AB, which they assumed stood for the male name Abraham, instead of her initials.

It didn't matter to Angel what arrangements had been made with regard to her father's estate. What she had depended on was gone—her father's wisdom and sound advice, his ability to share with her the sense of the ridiculous, and a feeling of belonging to someone very special. Angel had lost the person who meant the most to her in all the world. Nothing else seemed important to her, least of all anything that might have to do with her father's estate.

She reached into her small handbag, pulled out a finely embroidered lawn handkerchief and glanced up at Harry, praying that he wouldn't continue the scene much longer.

"I have provided each of you with copies of these documents, but since each one is several pages long and rather intricately worded in order to ensure the legality of them—" Harry interrupted himself and once again cleared his throat. "If you would like, I will try to cover the major points in each document."

Angel nodded, and Blake said, "If you would, Harry, I'm sure that will save a great deal of time."

"Yes, well, uh, I made some notes earlier, if I can just find them." He reached into his right breast pocket, then his left, found his glasses and picked up a single sheet of paper.

"The buy-sell agreement states that in the event something should happen to either Todd or Scott, the remaining party will buy out the other's interest, paying the money into the estate."

Blake leaned forward. "That is certainly fair, and I will be more than willing to buy out—" he glanced around at the woman seated in the chair next to him "—Angel's shares in the business."

Harry shifted restlessly in Scott's chair, wishing for the hundredth time that it was Scott having to sit there and explain to Blake Carlyle just what he and Todd thought they were going to accomplish by their ridiculous, at least in his opinion, strictures on their unsuspecting offspring.

"I'm afraid it isn't that easy, Blake. You see, that clause was written in the event that one of them survived the other. As you know, that isn't the case.

The clause on simultaneous deaths is a little more complicated."

Blake and Angel waited while Harry could feel the perspiration begin to dot his brow.

"What they decided, in the event that both of them should die at the same time, was to keep the shares in the family, so to speak."

"What family, Harry?" Blake asked in a suspicious voice.

"Uh, yours, Blake. Yours and Angel's."

"Could you be more explicit?"

"It's very simple, really. Todd and Scott decided that if anything happened to them they wanted to be sure that the shares would be used to the benefit of both of you. Therefore, they have left them in trust to any children born of the marriage of Blake Carlyle and Angel Bennington."

"What?" Blake and Angel said in unison.

"You can't be serious," Blake added.

"That is absolutely ridiculous!" Angel insisted. She glanced agitatedly at Blake for support. He was staring at Harry as though the man had suddenly stripped off his clothes and begun dancing nude on the desk. It was as though he wasn't sure what to do next—try to get him to sit down or try to find something with which to cover him.

Angel was suddenly reminded of a conversation she and her father had had a year or so ago.

Scott had dropped in unannounced at the large loft apartment Angel shared with two other artists. In addition to her roommates the place was filled with several other people, all talking and laughing at once. Angel had suggested she and Scott go downstairs to the corner café, where they could visit and catch up on the news.

"I can't understand how you can enjoy living such a communal life," Scott commented after the waiter had served them.

"Oh, but I love it, Papa. Now I am never lonely. I have my own family of artists, you see. We have so much in common, so much to share. For instance, all the excitement today is because Jean-Pierre sold one of his sculptures. It is marvelous to have friends who can appreciate what that means."

"What about a family of your own? Don't you want to have children?"

"But of course. I would love to have children someday—if I did not have to acquire a husband, as well." She wrinkled her nose in disdain.

"What's wrong with having a husband?"

"Everything. I do not want someone who will try to run my life. I love my independence too much. Besides, I have few wifely qualities, as we both know. When I get involved with my painting, I forget about the rest of the world." She shrugged. "So I accept my life as it is."

"You talk as though you never intend to marry."

"But, Papa, why should I? With the income from the trust and the sale of my paintings I have more than enough to live on."

Scott shook his head. "My darling daughter, despite what your mother might have drilled into your head all these years, there are other reasons to marry than for money."

Angel stared at him skeptically. "Name one."

Scott laughed and squeezed her hand. "Don't try to convince me of your cynicism. I know you too well. You are a romantic at heart."

"If you mean that I cry at touching movies, enjoy candlelit dinners, red roses and walks in the moonlight, then of course you're right. But, Papa, that has absolutely nothing to do with marriage. In fact, I should venture to point out the two are almost diametrically opposed." She took his hand and kissed the knuckles. "Why would anyone want to marry?"

"How about companionship?"

"I already have that without the emotional involvement that goes into making a relationship work. Suzanne, Michelle—they are like sisters to me, and Jean-Pierre is the brother I never had."

"And what if you fall in love with someone?"

"I would run, not walk, to the nearest exit. I have no intention of falling in love. I prefer my friendships. I do not want a passionate lover."

"Oh, Angel, I do worry about you, my love. You sound so cynical at such a young age. Your mother and I have much to answer for. Please understand that not every marriage turns out the way ours did."

"Yet you loved Mama very much."

"Yes. No one will ever be able to take her place in my heart."

"Then why did you allow her to leave?"

"Because she was unhappy. I loved her enough to want to see her happy, and if leaving me accomplished that goal, I was willing to do it."

"It did not make you happy for her to leave you."

"No, as a matter of fact, it didn't. You see, I not only lost her, but I lost you, as well."

"Oh, Papa, you never lost me. I have always been here for you."

"I know, my love, I know. But I won't always be here for *you* and I'd like to know that you are loved and cared for."

"No one can make those guarantees, Papa. I am fine, just fine. Please don't worry about me."

Obviously her father had ignored her admonishment. *Oh, Papa, how could you have suggested such a thing! You knew how I would feel about marrying anyone.* Angel looked at Harry. "You *are* serious, aren't you? Todd and Papa actually drew up papers saying that Blake and I are to marry?"

"I am afraid so," Harry muttered unhappily.

"I won't do it. The whole idea is preposterous."

"Yes," Harry agreed with heartfelt sympathy.

She glanced around at Blake. "Did you have

something to do with this?" Her tone was angrily accusing.

"Hardly," Blake responded with quiet emphasis. "If and when I marry I will choose my own wife." *And she will be nothing like you,* he added silently.

Blake pictured Marcia, tall and fashionably thin, her black hair swept back from her fine-featured face. He had been seeing her for more than two years. No two women could be more unalike. Marcia was calm and serene, sure of her position in life. She led an orderly existence and would be able to provide love, comfort and emotional security to his children if and when he chose to have a family.

In fact, if Blake were to point to the very antithesis of what he wanted in a wife, Angel would have made a very good example.

Not that he had anything against her looks. Although she was tiny, she certainly had all the attributes in the right places. But she was too flashy for his tastes with her bright hair and unusually dark-blue eyes. What he found even more offensive was the fact that she made no effort to play down her flamboyant coloring. Worn loose around her face, her hair glinted and shimmered, shooting sparks of fire whenever she moved. Every eye was drawn to her whenever she walked into a room.

However, it was her deceptive look of innocence that Blake found most irritating. Raised in France by that mother of hers—attending art classes in Paris by the time she was a teenager and living with a bunch of hippie-type artists—of course she was experienced, no doubt promiscuous, and he had the sudden urge to tell her to cut out that wide-eyed innocent look, that he, for one, wasn't buying her act.

He had no idea what their fathers had thought they were doing, but he certainly wasn't going to be saddled with a bohemian-type artist for a wife.

Blake straightened in his chair and gave Harry a level look. "What is the alternative regarding the shares?" he asked in a calm voice.

"That the corporation go public."

"What?" Blake couldn't believe what he was hearing.

"All the shares will be offered for sale on the stock market."

"You can't do that."

"No, I can't. But your fathers can. And that is exactly what they've instructed their executor, who by the way is me, to do as soon as the estates are settled."

"I don't believe this." Blake ran his hand through his hair in agitation. "Why didn't you tell me what they had planned, Harry?"

"In the first place, it would have been unethical. In the second place, I didn't think the provisions would ever be brought into play. And in the third place, I fully expected for them to have their little joke, then change it, fully enjoying the idea without ever letting either of you know anything about it."

Blake had been too busy during the days since the men had been killed to face the fact that they were truly gone. He had shoved his grieving aside, keeping busy making decisions, decisions he knew they would have wanted. But now the loss of his two mentors fell upon him and suddenly he felt crushed by the weight of the loss.

He missed them, and never so much as now, when, even from the grave, they were delighting in keeping him off balance—flexible, as they always called it. How many times had they admonished him to loosen up, lighten up, enjoy life, stop and smell the roses? And now they thought they had found a way to force him into the mold they wished for him.

How could you do this to me? he asked his dearly departed father and his father's best friend. *What have I ever done to deserve this sort of treatment from you?*

"Could you explain to me what's wrong with selling the shares?" Angel asked. "Won't that bring in a great deal of money?"

Blake slowly turned his head and looked disgustedly at Angel. "Yes, as a matter of fact, it would. But there's more to it than that. When a company goes public, you lose control. Shareholders come in, and they elect their own directors and officers and chairman. That company was built by our fathers and they wanted to retain complete control of the business. They did. They trained me to eventually take over. Now, if I don't agree to marry you and father your children, I will lose everything I've worked for. That probably doesn't mean a damned thing to you, does it?'' he asked bitterly.

Angel's own aversion to the outlandish suggestion began to pale when she recognized Blake's simmering reaction. He hadn't once raised his voice. If anything, he had become more quiet and controlled. Why did that make him appear dangerous? His black eyes burned with the intensity of his emotions, and Angel recognized there were hidden depths to the man.

Whatever could have caused their fathers to think that either one of them would agree to their preposterous plan?

She shook her head. This was too much, coming as it did directly on the heels of the shock of losing her father. She came to her feet. ''I will not do it, do you understand? I don't care about the stupid stock. I don't want a husband. If I did, I would marry a Frenchman—someone who knows about loving and laughter, not some stuffy American businessman who only becomes passionate reading a profit-and-loss statement!''

Angel burst into tears, the strain too much for her. Feeling thoroughly disgraced, she spun around and ran out of the room, slamming the library door behind her.

Blake sat there staring at the door for a moment, then he looked back at the man who had dropped the bombshell.

"All right, Harry," he said, settling back into his chair and folding his arms. "How do you propose we get out of this damned mess!"

Chapter Two

Angel stared out the wide, picturesque bay window of the library at the mist and fog. San Francisco, city of foghorns. She had never before been in the city without her father's presence for company.

During the three weeks since his death, Angel had put off working here in his library, but today she had forced herself to go through his papers and decide what to do with an accumulation of a lifetime.

Gladys, her father's housekeeper, had lit a fire in the fireplace, which had done much to dispel the cool dampness of the day, but nothing could hide the murkiness of the weather. Angel's thoughts flew to Paris and she wondered what Suzanne and Michelle were doing and if Jean-Pierre was busy on a new work of art.

Oh, how she missed her friends! There was something cool and brisk about San Francisco, and it wasn't just the weather. Angel knew so few people here. Harry checked on her regularly, calling and dropping by to share a meal with her. Surprisingly enough, they had found a mutual comfort in sharing stories of Scott and of Todd, and the emptiness of her life was at times held at bay.

She had heard nothing from Blake.

Harry had told her that Blake was in the midst of a reorganization of the company now that the two leaders were gone. The responsibility must be tremendous and she thought of Blake now, wondering how he managed to deal with the pressures of the company as well as his own personal loss.

Angel tried to remember everything her father had ever said about Blake but she could recall only small snatches and pieces of conversation. He considered Blake a genius at negotiating contracts and explaining the intricacies of their product in clear, understandable language. At one point he had mentioned that Todd was irritated at times with Blake's single-minded devotion to the business at the exclusion of everything else.

Why had Scott and Todd thought that a marriage between the two of them would work? Did her father feel that she needed to learn to be less independent? Did Todd think that marriage to Angel would teach

Blake that there were other things in life besides the business?

Similar thoughts had run around in her head for weeks along with the same question: why? *Oh, Papa, if you could only explain what you hoped to accomplish!*

Angel's painful introspection was interrupted by the ringing of the phone on the desk. She walked over, sat down and reached for the ringing instrument.

"H'lo?"

"Angel?"

The voice was deep with a slight rough edge that Angel found soothing and seductive.

"Yes?"

"This is Blake Carlyle."

She gripped the phone harder, recognizing a tightness in the pit of her stomach. Now that he was finally in contact with her, she felt a slight sense of panic that she couldn't explain.

"Yes?"

There was a silence, then a sigh. "I'm sorry I haven't called you sooner. How have you been?"

"As well as could be expected, I suppose."

"Do you have plans for this evening?"

"No."

"Would you like to have dinner with me?"

The thought of seeing him again caused a slight quivering within her. Was she scared of him? Surely not. Angel Bennington was afraid of no man. But she recognized and admitted that she was afraid of what he represented in her life—change. Everything was changing so rapidly for her, and he was a part of it.

"That would be nice, Blake. When?"

"I will be there as soon after seven as I can make it, if that's all right with you."

"Fine, I'll see you then."

She heard the slight click of the phone and a dial tone before lowering the phone to the cradle.

He sounded so decisive, so used to issuing invitations—and commands, perhaps? Was he also used to being obeyed? More than likely. Despite herself, Angel was becoming intrigued with the enigmatic Blake Carlyle.

Angel's love for color was obvious in her wardrobe, and the dress she chose to wear for dinner was no exception. It was a lime green, with full, sheer sleeves, a V-neck and a full skirt that swirled around her shapely legs. Glancing at her image in the mirror she tugged at the neckline, frowning slightly. It was a little lower than she preferred, but she shrugged philosophically. Blake would probably not even notice.

Blake noticed.

He was waiting in the hallway when Angel came down the stairway. Gladys, whom he had known since he was a boy, had let him in and gone to tell

Angel of his arrival. The lights from the chandelier glinted off her fiery curls, which tumbled around her face and shoulders in casual disarray. He wondered if she had deliberately set out to appear provocative or whether it came second nature to her.

Angel couldn't help but notice how striking Blake appeared in the black suit he wore. With his ink-black hair and eyes and bronzed skin, he could have played the role of tempter for Satan. From the grim expression he wore, however, Blake didn't appear to be looking forward to an evening with her.

She placed a small hand at her midriff in an unconscious gesture, forcing herself to relax. She smiled.

Angel's smile caught Blake off guard. A sweet shyness fought with the overall impression of sophistication, a contradiction he found confusing. Her first comments added further to the confusion.

"I appreciate your willingness to see me again after that awful scene I caused a few weeks ago. I was dreading having to apologize in a letter or over the phone." She stopped a few steps from him. "I hope you will forgive my rudeness. I said some really unforgivable things and I'm sorry."

One corner of Blake's mouth lifted in a half smile. He was totally disarmed by her honesty. He took the hand she held out to him and squeezed it gently. "You don't owe me an apology, Angel. We were both under a tremendous amount of pressure that day. Harry should have understood we weren't ready to hear what he had to say at that time."

Her smile widened as she tilted her head back to look at him. "Oh, I wouldn't have been ready to hear that I was supposed to marry someone at *any* time, particularly someone I don't even know."

He was fascinated by the dancing light that appeared in her eyes. She had such an expressive face. Blake continued to hold her hand and stare at her.

"Will I need a jacket, do you suppose?"

His glance fell to her dress. From his vantage point he had a bird's-eye view of her shoulders and the full curve of her breasts.

"Definitely." He forced himself to look away from the enticing view.

Angel took a light jacket from the coatroom and with hard-earned nonchalance handed it to Blake, then turned her back to him. Once again he was presented with an unimpeded view.

Blake stiffened. What the hell was she trying to do, seduce him? He held the jacket while she slipped her arms into the sleeves, slipping her hair to fall outside of the coat. Blake was reminded of Yvette and her teasing, provocative manner.

Angel was just like her mother; anyone could see that. Now that she would inherit everything that Scott had amassed in his lifetime, he was certain she would quit playing at being an artist and enjoy a life of flitting from one resort area to the other.

Not until I get what I want from her, he reminded himself.

"Shall we go?" he asked politely.

For a few moments Blake had almost seemed human, but he had quickly resumed all the animation of a robot. That ability might be great at poker or at a conference table, but Angel found it rather grim.

"Of course," she said in her most regal terms. *What a fun evening this is going to be.*

They drove down to Fisherman's Wharf and entered one of the restaurants on the water. They were seated at a small table in front of a wide picture window that overlooked the bay. Spotlights picked up the small whitecaps that danced occasionally on top of the wake of a passing boat. Angel was surprised that anyone would venture out on the bay after dark.

The meal was delicious but Blake's mind seemed to be somewhere else. He was probably still at the office mentally going over documents and figures, Angel decided. She wondered what it would take to gain his attention and decided to find out.

Folding her hands lightly under her chin, Angel leaned on her elbows and smiled across the table at him. The soft candlelight cast shadows across his face, making him look even more mysterious than normal.

"Are you dating anyone, Blake?"

He glanced at her over the top of his wineglass, startled at the personal question. "Why do you ask?"

"Oh, I just wondered. I suppose I'm surprised that you aren't already married, which would have taken care of the situation in which we presently find ourselves."

"The same holds true for you. Why aren't *you* married?"

She smiled. "I don't like ties."

I just bet you don't, he thought caustically. "Actually I am seeing someone at the moment—Marcia Sinclair."

"What is she like?"

"Tall, slender, beautiful." He eyed her thoughtfully, then took another swallow of wine.

The opposite of me. "Why haven't you married her?"

"There was no rush. We have plenty of time." He paused, hearing what he had said. "At least, I thought we did," he added bitterly.

"As far as I'm concerned, you have all the time in the world." She gave him her most innocent smile, but he met it with a frown.

"I have had several attorneys going over the papers Harry drew up, trying to find a way out of this situation."

"And?"

"And, short of litigation, which would be costly

and lengthy and would still not guarantee the results we want, there is nothing we can do."

"I see."

"Do you? Do you care anything about anybody but yourself and your own pleasures?"

"Of course I do!"

"I can't understand why your father disliked me so much that he would bribe me to marry you. I suppose he figured that was the only way he could get you married off."

Angel could feel the anger building within her. She smiled—a small, secret smile. "It works both ways, you know. Perhaps I am being bribed to marry you. Perhaps our fathers felt that no one else would have you, either."

A dull wash of red suddenly flooded Blake's cheeks, and his dark eyes blazed with fury.

Aha. So there are some feelings rumbling around inside that calm exterior, Angel decided with a certain amount of satisfaction.

"Is that what you think?"

"What? You are asking me for my thoughts? How unusual of you. I was certain you did not care a fig for what I think about anything."

"Do you think I had any idea they were planning something so insane?" he asked incredulously.

"I have no more reason to suppose you knew anything about their plans than you have for thinking that I knew about them. However, that hasn't seemed to stop you from jumping to the most ridiculous conclusions."

"Ridiculous?"

"Well, aren't they? Why in the world would you think that I would prefer to marry some stranger and move halfway around the world to live with him and furnish him with children?" She tilted her head slightly, a small, amused smile hovering on her face. "Unless, of course, I'm missing something very essential." She glanced at him from underneath her lashes. "Are you very good in bed, perhaps?"

He stared at the young woman sitting demurely across the table from him. The soft candlelight picked up fiery glints of color in her hair, enhanced the slightly apricot color of her cheeks and reflected all the innocence of a saint in her eyes.

In a low tone, Blake gritted out, "My prowess or lack of prowess in bed is certainly not the issue here."

Angel tilted her head, obviously considering the matter. "Well, I wouldn't be so quick to discount it, if I were you." She studied him consideringly. "I really think you need to advertise all of your positive qualities. I hardly see a woman falling for your wit and charm." She paused, her gaze limpid. "Of course, you have a certain amount of good looks that some people might find attractive. I've always preferred blond men, myself," she added with deliberate reluctance, as though uncertain whether she might offend him with her honesty.

"The issue at the moment has nothing to do with my attributes as a marriage partner."

"Well, you're in luck, then."

"Angel—" His voice had a certain threatening overtone.

"Yes?"

How did she do it? How could she sit there looking so innocent and unworldly while making the most outrageous comments? Blake took a deep breath, slowly exhaled and forced himself to relax. Perhaps she wasn't doing it on purpose. Life was different in France. How could he hold her responsible for her upbringing?

He reached over and took her hand. "Angel, I'm sorry. I'm not handling this conversation very well, I know. You'll have to excuse me. This whole situation has been something of a shock to me. I'm really not handling it well."

"I understand."

"Thank you. I realize that you had no more to do with it than I did."

"That's true."

"And you have no more interest in marrying me than I have in marrying you."

"Agreed."

"Fine." He sat back in his chair after patting her hand. It was unfortunate for Angel's peace of mind that in his sudden relief at her acknowledgment of what he had been trying to say, Blake smiled at her. His smile was dazzling. For just a moment Angel had trouble catching her breath. When he wasn't frowning, when he forgot to be serious, Blake Carlyle was devastatingly attractive.

Angel stared at him, bemused by the implications of her discovery. "Blake?"

"Yes?"

"*Are* you good in bed?"

"Angel!"

"I just wondered."

"Have you heard a word that I have said?"

"Mmm-hmm." She smiled.

Why did her smile unnerve him so? He got the distinct impression that she was playing with him, as a mischievous cat might play with a harried mouse.

"However," he added slowly, "I do not want the company to go public."

She blinked uncertainly. Hadn't they already resolved that issue?

"But you just said—"

"I just said that I have no more interest in marrying you than you have in marrying me. That doesn't mean that I don't have every intention of marrying you."

From feeling fully in control of a situation to feeling tossed in the middle of a swirling tornado, Angel stared at Blake in total disbelief.

"You're serious, aren't you?"

"Absolutely."

"But you don't even know me."

"I am well aware of that, but I want you to understand that I have no intention of allowing the company to go public and I will do whatever I have to do to keep it in my control."

"Even to marrying me."

"Yes."

"But what about Marcia?"

"What about her?"

"Don't you love Marcia?"

"My feelings are totally irrelevant. I do not make decisions based on feelings, let me assure you."

He sat there staring at her implacably, and Angel got a glimpse of the ruthlessness that had made him so successful.

"What about *my* feelings?"

"I would like to spare your feelings as much as possible."

"How big of you," she muttered ungraciously.

"That's why I am proposing that you delay your return to France and give us an opportunity to get better acquainted before the wedding."

"Before the wedding! Blake, there will be no wedding."

"Harry said there was no time limit placed on the marriage and on producing the family."

"I wonder how they missed planning that, as well?" she asked bitterly of no one in particular.

"You've already made it clear that you have no intention of marrying anyone else, so any plans we make would not interfere with your future that I can see."

"Not that I'm agreeing to anything, but for the sake of discussion, let's suppose I agreed to your suggestion. Would I be able to live in France after the marriage?"

The waiter appeared and refilled their glasses, and Blake was amused to notice that Angel quickly took a drink from her refilled glass. She obviously wasn't as composed as she wished him to believe.

He shook his head. "Not right away. If you will recall the terms, it isn't enough that we are married. We will need to have at least one child." He raised one eyebrow slightly. "We would need to live intimately for a while at least."

She set the glass down. "I don't believe this. You don't care that I don't want to marry you."

"Of course I care. It just doesn't change anything. I have no intention of rushing you into anything. We have time—time to let you grow adjusted to life here in San Francisco, time to spend together, time for you to meet my friends and business associates and to make friends of your own." His mouth widened into a mischievous grin. "You might even grow to like me, which would be a definite improvement over our present relationship."

"On the contrary, Blake, *darling*," she drawled. "It's obvious that I am not your idea of a mate any more than you are mine."

He nodded. "True."

"So perhaps it is possible that you will even grow to like me."

"The idea does show considerable merit." He glanced at his watch. "Are you ready to go?"

Angel glanced at her empty wineglass in surprise. She'd certainly drunk her wine in a hurry, but it had left her with an uncomfortably muddled feeling. She had too much to think about, and she needed time—and distance from Blake—to get her thoughts in order.

The drive home was silent, and Angel studied the passing streets as though determined to find her way around San Francisco as soon as possible. The mist and fog had cleared and she could see the stars twinkling above. She wished the mist and fog in her head would clear as readily. Never had she felt so confused.

Blake wondered what she was thinking but was afraid to ask. He wasn't at all certain he was ready to listen to one of her candid responses.

When they reached her home, Blake helped Angel out of the car, walked her up the steps, opened the door to the large home and escorted her inside. He slipped her jacket from her shoulders and she turned around and stared up at him uncertainly.

"Would you like some coffee?"

"No, thanks. I need to go. I'll call you tomorrow. There's a party at the end of the week that would give you an opportunity to get acquainted. Why don't you plan to go with me?"

"But what about Marcia?"

"Would you please quit worrying about Marcia? She's none of your business. You'll just have to take my word for it that I will handle Marcia."

"All right."

She looked like a young girl standing there in her sophisticated gown, and without giving his actions much thought Blake placed his hands on her shoulders, cupping them, and leaned down to kiss her mouth. Had he been questioned at that point, he would have explained that his only intention was to give her a quick peck on the lips. He was never certain later how the kiss changed to become something more.

It definitely became something more. Angel moved closer to him, her arms slowly creeping up around his neck, her mouth fitting his so perfectly that it seemed to be made for him. When he felt her pressed against him Blake seemed to forget who she was and why they were together. Instead, his body began to signal a definite attraction to the woman in his arms and he tightened his hold, pulling her even closer to him.

Her mouth parted slightly, her tongue flicking mischievously against his sensual lower lip, and their mouths suddenly merged, their tongues lightly fencing.

Angel couldn't understand what was happening to her. Never had she responded to a man in such a manner. Everywhere their bodies touched seemed to be lit with a flame. She was quivering with reaction to his closeness. She could feel his arousal and was vaguely aware of the unconscious expertise he brought to the art of kissing.

Angel was way over her head. She knew so little about men—had never been tempted to learn—and now she was getting all her lessons rolled up into one dynamite package.

Blake's hand unconsciously searched for and found Angel's breast, its warmth causing his fingers to tingle as he softly slid his fingers around its fullness. It was only when he heard Angel's soft moan that he realized what he was doing.

My God! Are you out of your mind? This is Angel Bennington you're caressing. Slowly he withdrew his hand, but his lips seemed to have a mind of their own as they continued to possess hers in a timeless merging.

It was Angel who finally broke the contact. She unlocked the hold she had around his neck and bonelessly slid her arms down his chest. She backed up until her hand was on the ornate front door of her father's home. "Good night, Blake," she managed to murmur.

He stood there, wondering if San Francisco was being threatened by another quake. Why were his knees so shaky and why did he have this intense urge to gather her back into his arms and carry her up that long, winding staircase to the first available bed?

"Good night, Angel," he managed to mutter.

Blake got back into his car and drove off, trying to understand what had happened to him. He had been with many women, but he had never reacted to one so intensely before. Angel Bennington? Was he out of his mind? He tried to think of Marcia but couldn't seem to remember what she looked like. Instead, all he could see were large dark-blue eyes and flaming-red hair.

The strain of the past few weeks had finally caught up with him. He must be losing his mind.

Chapter Three

Blake Carlyle paced back and forth in front of Harrison Tyler's overflowing desk. Harry watched him with concern. Blake rarely showed so much agitation. One of his most noticeable traits was his ability to hide what he was feeling. But not today.

Blake had pulled his tie loose from its normally pristine knot and his coat had long since been tossed on a nearby chair.

"Dammit, Harry, you've got to help me get out of this situation!"

Since his remarks had been more or less of the same nature for the past twenty minutes, Harry no longer felt obligated to respond. There was nothing he could say that would in any way alleviate the problem.

"A marriage between Angel and me would be a disaster. I thought I could do it, but I can't." He whirled around. "You saw what happened at the Montgomery's the other night."

Harry stared at him in surprise. "I thought Angel was very well received at the Montgomery party, Blake. Everyone seemed to enjoy her very much."

"She practically caused a riot in that dress. Of course they enjoyed her. There was quite a lot of Angel on display to enjoy!"

"There was nothing wrong with her dress, Blake. I'm sure it is very fashionable in Paris and the color certainly brightened up the room."

"But that's just my point. We aren't in Paris and none of the other women were dressed to call so much attention to themselves."

"Such as Marcia."

"Right. Marcia is a good example. Marcia always dresses with dignity and decorum."

Harry smiled. "While Angel dresses with a vibrant vitality that draws the eye of every man in the room. Scott would have been proud of her. I thought of him often that night. He would have loved to be there showing her off to all his friends."

"Did you hear what she said to Judge Lewis?"

"No."

"That if he didn't cut down on the amount of liquor he was putting away and lose fifty pounds or more, the next funeral she attended would probably be his!''

Harry laughed. "I would love to have seen the old goat's face. What did he say?"

"He loved it. Said she sounded just like her father but was a hell of a lot better looking. He also said his wife was always harping at him about his eating and drinking habits but had never been quite so descriptive."

"So he wasn't offended."

"Thank God. But can you see Marcia saying something so outrageous to a person she had just met? Or even someone she has known for years, for that matter?"

"No, I can't."

"Neither can I, and I find that very reassuring. During the entire evening I never knew what Angel was going to say or do. She seems to delight in the unexpected."

"Blake, try to understand Angel. She has an unusual background. She has never been part of the social scene with which you are familiar. It was that very difference that Scott always encouraged—the honesty, the candidness."

"That's just great. Then why did he expect me, of all people, to marry her?"

"Perhaps he thought you would each contribute something to the other."

Blake sank down into a nearby chair. "The only

thing she's contributed to me so far is a colossal headache." He rubbed his forehead wearily. "There's got to be another way out of this mess."

Harry sat watching him for a few moments. "You know, Blake, you really surprise me. When I talked to you last week you sounded determined to marry her and spoke of it almost like a business merger. I can't remember ever having seen you this emotional about a business problem before."

Blake slowly raised his head and stared at Harry in surprise. He was quiet and Harry waited patiently for him to think about his remark.

What had caused the change? Blake asked himself. It had started with that kiss he and Angel had shared. The kiss had stirred up emotions Blake hadn't known he possessed. And he didn't like them. Not at all. He had been honest when he had told Angel that he never considered his feelings when he made a decision. So why were his emotions fighting to take control now?

What in the world was he afraid of, anyway? So what if she was different from every other woman he knew? The fact remained that he needed to marry her in order to get on with the life he had planned.

The other fact that she had made clear to him was that if he was determined they were to marry, then she would decide when, as well as the rules of the marriage. She also made it clear to him that she would not be one of those typical executive wives, that she didn't have the time to socialize nor the desire to do so. She wanted freedom to come and go as she pleased and to paint, especially to paint, without any hindrance from him.

She pointed out that he didn't want a wife, anyway. He was only looking for a brood mare. She had never intended to be a wife, either to him or to anyone else, but since their fathers had come up with their scheme she might consider having his child in order to comply with their wishes.

One of the things that was eating at Blake was that he no longer felt in control of his life. He distrusted the feeling of being at someone else's mercy. Especially someone as unpredictable and capricious as Angel Bennington.

He looked up in time to see Harry unobtrusively glancing at his watch.

Blake stood up. "Sorry to take up so much of your time with my problems, Harry. I'll get out of here and let you get back to work."

Harry came around the desk and shook hands with Blake. "It will all work out, Blake—I know it will. You and Angel share a heritage of sorts. Your fathers meant well. Why don't you give the idea a chance?"

"I don't have much of a choice. My hands are tied. Angel hasn't definitely decided to marry me. I feel like such a fool—left dangling by a woman that normally I would avoid. She's probably enjoying the sense of power all of this gives her."

"Do you really think so?"

"The truth is I have no idea. I can't figure her out at all. She doesn't seem to care about money or social prestige, things most women are looking for. She seems to take her art seriously, but there's not much of a future in that field that I can see."

"Scott said she's quite good. Have you ever seen her work?"

"No. But if it keeps her busy and content, what difference does it make whether any of it sells or not? Being Scott Bennington's sole survivor, she'll never have to earn a penny for the rest of her life."

Harry walked him to the door. "Keep me posted on what happens. I intend to give the bride away, you know."

"There's plenty of time to make plans for that. First we have to establish that there's going to *be* a bride."

Blake closed the door to Harry's office and nodded absently to Glenda, Harry's secretary, a brisk, efficient young woman who had secretly admired Blake Carlyle for years. She often wondered what it would take for him ever to notice her. She had a hunch that even if she stripped down to the bare essentials he would give her the same absentminded nod whenever he was in to see Harry. Glenda sighed. Those looks—that body—and the mind of a computer. What a waste.

Glancing at his watch, Blake decided to drive by

Angel's home before going on to his office. He hadn't talked with her since he had taken her home from the party the other night. On that occasion he had not made the mistake of kissing her good-night.

So I'm physically attracted to her, he admitted to himself. *So what?* With her background and obvious experience it wasn't surprising that she would be able to project a seductive, alluring image. Their fathers had still pictured her as an innocent child. As a matter of fact, she managed to project the epitome of innocence when it was politic for her to do so. No doubt that was the side of her their fathers had always seen. They probably figured she needed protecting and had chosen him for the job. That was a laugh. Who was going to protect him from her?

He drove into the long driveway and pulled up in front of the large home. Blake wondered what she intended to do with the place. Benningtons had owned the property for several generations. She could make quite a lot of money if she decided to sell. The thought irked him. Acquiring more money certainly wasn't a goal of hers.

What did she want? Angel seemed to attract people with ease, her open, vivacious temperament drawing people to her. Blake noticed that even the women at the party had enjoyed visiting with her. Perhaps it was because she showed such an interest in everyone. She wasn't a flirt, he forced himself to admit. But when anyone had eyed her with a lascivious gleam in his eye, Blake had felt a sudden urge to deck him.

He couldn't understand his reactions at all.

The housekeeper opened the door on the second ring.

"Good afternoon, Gladys. Is Angel here?"

"Yes, she is, Blake. She's upstairs painting, if you want to go on up."

Blake took the stairs two at a time, ignoring the eagerness in which he went in search of Angel. Opening the door to the room Scott had converted into a studio for Angel some years ago, Blake paused. Angel did not look up from her concentrated study of the canvas in front of her. She painstakingly applied dashes of color, then stepped back and studied the effect.

Angel had on an old, paint-spattered smock and a pair of jeans that she must have had for years. They had been washed so much they were almost white and their snug fit suggested they were bought when she was even smaller than her present size. Her hair was pulled into a loose, lopsided topknot, with tendrils of curls falling across her forehead and cheeks. Her hair must have bothered her at one point— she wore a streak of azure blue just above her eyebrows that accented the deep color of her eyes.

She glanced up suddenly, startled at the knowledge she was no longer alone.

"I'm sorry, Blake, I didn't hear you come in."

"I didn't mean to disturb you."

Angel chuckled, and the sound touched a chord inside him, making him quiver. "Oh, you didn't. I'm about finished, anyway. I came up here early this morning, to get the morning light, and somehow couldn't drag myself away." She glanced up at the giant skylight overhead. "The light is rotten now."

"Have you eaten?"

She shook her head, busy cleaning her brushes.

"That's stupid, Angel. You need to eat. You've lost weight since you came."

"I know," she murmured. "I haven't felt much like eating lately."

He walked over and placed his hands on her small shoulders, kneading the muscles under his strong fingers. "Why don't you let me take you somewhere for lunch?"

"No, that's okay. Gladys said she had sandwiches made up for me whenever I was ready to eat. You're welcome to join me," she added, glancing over her shoulder.

She knew Blake was wasting his time trying to help her relax. She tensed up every time she saw him. Angel had no idea how she would have reacted to the man if she hadn't known her father had wanted her to marry him. She remembered the number of times Scott had suggested she fly over to the States when Blake was home. Now that she understood his motives better she recognized how much of his comments during the past few years were in the way of matchmaking. He and Todd may have first thought of it as a joke, but Angel was convinced her father had later decided it was a good idea.

But Angel didn't want to get married. And if she had ever decided she might like the idea, she would have preferred to pick her own mate. She had forced herself, however, to face the fact that she was really being given very little choice in the matter. Of course, arranged marriages were not unheard of in Europe, particularly when business interests were so intertwined, as was the case with the Benningtons and the Carlyles.

But marry Blake Carlyle? Oh, please! Take as a husband someone as serious, reserved, cold and unemotional as Blake? *He wasn't cold the night he kissed you,* she reminded herself. Far from it. Angel had felt as though she were being held against a fiery furnace, his ardor and obvious arousal singeing her.

What a contradiction he was.

Angel carefully placed her brushes in their proper place and turned around. Blake continued to stand there, so that she was effectively pinned between him and her easel.

"When are you going to marry me, Angel?"

It would be hard to decide who was the more surprised at the question, Blake or Angel. Setting the date for a wedding wasn't what he had been thinking about. What had filled his mind was the soft floral scent that seemed to surround her, how small she seemed next to him and how childlike she appeared with her hair worn like that.

Angel forced herself to face him, then wished she hadn't. His black eyes seemed to reflect her image, his serious face studying her intensely, and Angel found she was having trouble remembering to breathe.

Angel deftly sidestepped him, needing space. She almost ran to the door, then forced herself to take each step down the staircase, concentrating on placing her feet carefully while searching for an answer to Blake's question. She needed more time. Hadn't he told her the night they discussed marriage that there was no rush? Why was he pushing her now?

Blake followed her. He watched as she darted down the hallway to the kitchen. Angel seemed to be constantly moving, like a sprite dashing through the halls. He wandered into the small dining alcove, knowing that sooner or later she would appear in there to eat.

Eventually Angel entered the room carrying a plate of sandwiches and slowly approached the table where Blake waited. She sat down across from him.

"I can't marry you right away, Blake. It's too soon. I'm still trying to get through each day...trying to adjust to the fact that Papa isn't just a phone call away."

"I can understand that, and I'm not trying to rush

you. It's just that I need to make some plans for the business and thought we could work out some sort of schedule that would benefit both of us."

I can't believe the man. He's planning to work his marriage into his schedule like a dental appointment. "Could we announce our engagement and wait for a few months, so that everyone, including us, could get used to the idea?"

"That sounds reasonable."

She almost laughed. Obviously reasonable suggestions deserved his stamp of approval. Why did she have a strong urge to be unreasonable just to see his reaction? She quelled the impulse.

Angel watched with fascination as Blake pulled a pen and small notebook from his inner coat pocket. He was treating their discussion like any other business meeting, preparing to take notes. She looked away, refusing to meet his eye.

"I would need to go back to France sometime before we married. As you know, I left in a rush and I have several matters to conclude over there." She paused, waiting for his reaction.

He nodded, seemingly satisfied with the suggestion. "The situation doesn't need to be permanent, you know. After we're married you would be free to spend most of your time in France, if you prefer."

Why did his calm, logical statement cause a constriction in her chest? She was afraid she knew. Angel was very much afraid that marriage to Blake Carlyle was going to be a painful experience for her.

"It isn't enough that we marry, Blake. We have to produce at least one child." She could feel the heat in her cheeks and prayed that he wouldn't notice.

"I've thought of that." As a matter of fact, he had spent several restless nights lately thinking about having children with Angel, having her in his bed, waking up to find her next to him each morning. "One child would be enough to fulfill the stipulation."

"And what do you propose to do with him...or her...if I should decide to return to France? Would I be allowed to take the child with me?"

"Of course. You and your father managed a close relationship even though you lived apart. There's no reason to suppose I couldn't travel back and forth, and you would be free to travel, as well."

Oh, he had it all figured out—coolly, logically, unemotionally. She wondered how he did it. He was saying he could live with her, make love to her, then calmly ship her off after their child was born. Could she live like that? But could she deny him the business that he felt was his birthright? How would she feel if someone told her she could never paint again? No doubt he felt as tied to the business as she did to her art.

Besides, it was quite possible that after living with

such a cold person she would be delighted to move away from him, particularly if she had a child.

A child. She had consciously refused to consider the full implications of the situation until now. Angel had never thought of herself as maternal, assuming that, like her mother, she was too self-centered and wrapped up in her career to want a family. Now she wasn't so sure—particularly if she had a boy with Blake's dark eyes and hair. She had a sudden mental picture of a solemn little boy looking up at her, waiting to be loved and cuddled. Perhaps that was what Blake had missed as a child—the warm affection of a doting parent.

"Shall we go ahead and set a date for the wedding?"

She thought for a few moments. It was the end of January. "How about April or May?"

He nodded. "What sort of wedding do you want? A large one, I suppose."

"Oh, no. Please. It isn't as though we are doing anything more than complying with the stipulations made. I'd much prefer a small, private ceremony."

Blake nodded once again, making notations in a bold, slashing script.

Angel had a sudden insane urge to laugh at the preposterous discussion. How had she ever managed to get involved in such a situation?

He glanced up. "You will tell your other men friends, then, that you are to be married? I don't want there to be any doubt that any child you have is mine."

Angel felt as though he'd doubled his fist and struck her in the stomach. Her men friends. Is that what he thought about her?

Blake saw her delicate color fade and wished he could cut out his tongue. Surely he could have phrased the request more tactfully. "I'm sorry, I didn't mean that the way it sounded."

"Of course you did, Blake, and it's quite understandable. So far I've been able to find homes for all of my children when my indiscretions have caught up with me, but to be on the safe side I'll curtail my extensive sexual activities for the next few months, so there'll be no doubt that you are the father of my next one."

Angel delivered her outrageous response in a controlled, no-nonsense voice. In fact, it was carefully modulated to sound as calm and objective as Blake's had been.

"You have other children?" Blake asked in disbelief.

"Oh, yes," she responded nonchalantly. "A litter of them, it seems at times. I do try to stay in contact with them on a regular basis, though, and never overlook sending monthly checks for their upkeep." She leaned toward him confidentially. "I wouldn't want you to think I'm irresponsible. Heavens, no. And I want to assure you right now that any child you and

I have will receive my full attention and support. After all, he or she will have the responsibility of the corporation someday." She paused, trying to hide the bitterness that tried to overwhelm her. "The corporation, after all, is what is important. Why, we're all sacrificing our lives to it."

Blake peered at the young woman across from him incredulously. Could she possibly be serious? She certainly didn't look as though she were joking. As a matter of fact, she seemed to be very calm and offhand, except for a slight flush to her cheeks.

"How many children do you have, Angel?"

"I've lost count."

"Angel!"

"Yes?"

"Why in the world would you make such a ridiculous statement? I know you don't have any children."

"How do you know?"

"In the first place, your father would have told me."

"I didn't tell my father everything."

"In the second place, you are too young to have had 'a litter' of children, as you put it."

"I could have started young, you know."

"Angel..." Her earnest expression was so innocent that it stopped him from further comment. Why in the world was he arguing with her about it? Once again she had managed to disconcert him with one of her outrageous remarks. She seemed to enjoy doing that.

"I apologize for my boorish comment earlier. It is none of my business to whom you have made love. I am sure you would not be so crude as to bring up my past to me."

"I wouldn't?"

"Of course not."

She thought about that for a moment. "How about if I just ask about one or two?"

"Angel!"

"We could trade stories, if you'd like."

"Never mind." He glanced down at the list in front of him. "Would you like to have a church wedding?"

She thought about that for a moment. In all likelihood, this would be her one and only marriage. Perhaps she was like her father. He had never stopped loving Yvette, had always shown Angel's mother nothing but consideration, and Angel could remember particular instances when her mother had deserved considerably less.

Angel studied Blake thoughtfully. Was she even capable of loving someone in the same manner? She had a hunch that Blake was capable of evoking intense feeling in her. She had always considered herself to be even tempered and good-natured. Why then could she become so incensed with him? And why did his kiss set her on fire, provoking all sorts of feelings that had never surfaced before?

"Angel?"

She smiled at him mistily. "Yes?"

Blake sighed. She could be exasperating to the extreme. "Do you want to be married in a church or in a civil ceremony?" he repeated with strained patience.

"Oh! I would prefer a church ceremony."

"You would?" he asked in surprise. He would have guessed that a civil ceremony would have sufficed for her. Blake wasn't at all sure how he felt about it. He was trying not to feel anything. They had decided to go ahead with marriage plans and he was determined to be as objective as possible. He refused to allow himself to picture Angel as his wife. There was plenty of time to face that step.

"Do you have anyone in particular that you want to include in the wedding invitations?"

A mischievous grin appeared on her face. "I don't suppose you want any of my lovers to attend," she said softly. "Although perhaps you would prefer to meet them and discuss my more, uh, intimate preferences with you." She smiled such a demure smile that he could have spanked her.

"You're really not that amusing, Angel. I doubt that you have had all that many lovers, anyway." As he said it, Blake realized that he believed it. She could not project such an air of untouched innocence if she were as experienced as she tried to make him believe. He wondered why he found the thought reassuring.

Blake studied his notes for a few minutes in silence and Angel wondered what else was left to discuss.

"The engagement party," Blake muttered as though reading her mind, and she started.

"What engagement party?"

He looked up at her in surprise. "Surely you would prefer to treat this matter confidentially, wouldn't you?"

She nodded, uncertain of his point.

"If we are going to have a quiet wedding, we will have to make our engagement very public so that there will be no question but that we met again after all these years, fell in love and decided to marry."

"Do you really believe anyone is going to buy that story?" she asked skeptically.

"Of course."

"Even Marcia?"

"I will deal with Marcia without any assistance from you." He pocketed the notebook and pen and stood up. "I believe that covers most of the details at the moment. When do you intend to return to France?"

"I will need to be here at least two more weeks."

He pulled out a small calendar from another coat pocket and studied it. "We'll have the party a week from Saturday." He glanced at her. "Will that give you enough time?"

"Enough time for what?"

"To find a suitable gown to wear."

"I suppose that depends on your definition of suitable. I'm sure I'll find something."

He nodded, wishing he could suggest that she allow Marcia to accompany her shopping, but he didn't believe either woman would be particularly receptive to the idea, especially after he told Marcia the reason for the shopping expedition.

Blake wasn't looking forward to breaking the news to Marcia that their relationship was going to end. There was no doubt in Blake's mind that she would accept his news, but since he couldn't tell her the real reason, he knew that pretending he had fallen in love with someone would call for his best acting abilities. He didn't want to hurt Marcia, but he owed his loyalty to Angel now that she was going to be his wife.

Negotiating a business deal had never been so complicated. How had his father and Scott ever thought a marriage between the two of them would enrich their lives? It was already causing serious complications to his entire life-style. Blake had a strong hunch matters were only going to get worse.

Angel politely walked him to the door, where he paused and glanced down at her.

"I want you to know I appreciate your willingness to go along with this insane idea."

"I'm not doing it for you, Blake. I am doing it for my father. He would never have suggested something that would harm me. Obviously he felt we would both benefit from a marriage. My father was an astute man and he knew both of us extremely well. Despite the fact that I cannot envision why he thought a marriage between the two of us would work, I trust his judgment implicitly."

Blake stared down into the dark-blue depths of Angel's eyes, seeing the honest clarity of her expression for the first time. How could he have lost track of the fact that she was Scott Bennington's daughter? Perhaps it was because she looked so much like her mother. He was ashamed to recognize how much he had judged her because of her mother, meanwhile ignoring her father's obvious influence in her life.

He ran his hand along the nape of her neck and tilted her head up to him. "It will all work out, Angel."

Never had she heard his voice so gentle. She almost believed him. And when he lowered his mouth to hers, his kiss was softly reassuring.

For the first time since her father had died, Angel didn't feel quite so alone in the world.

Chapter Four

Blake's way of life was based on orderly concepts. After arranging for the engagement party to be held at one of the local downtown hotels and having his secretary prepare a list of friends and business associates for him to designate whom to invite, he turned his attention to the next item on his agenda—Marcia.

He hadn't seen much of her since he had taken over the company, which hadn't come as a surprise to her, he was sure. Marcia was the daughter of a very powerful, very astute businessman and she understood the pressures under which Blake thrived. She lived at home with her father, playing hostess to his friends and associates. In her spare time she did various volunteer work. Marcia would make someone a perfect wife. Unfortunately for Blake, his situation had changed too drastically for him to be able to ask her to marry him.

While driving Marcia to the opera one evening that week, Blake asked himself why he had never proposed marriage to Marcia. She was everything he had ever wanted in a wife—intelligent, attractive, understanding. Blake supposed he had taken their relationship for granted.

Now it was too late. How did he go about explaining to her that he was going to marry someone else?

Blake's mind kept wandering throughout the evening's performance. When it was over he took Marcia to his apartment. He realized that once he and Angel were married, they would live in the large home he'd grown up in, but his penthouse suite was convenient to his offices and he fully intended to keep it.

As they rode up in the elevator Marcia was telling him about some interesting gossip she had heard and he tried to concentrate on what she was saying. Obviously he didn't do a good job.

"What's wrong, Blake?" she asked, interrupting her story. "You seem distracted."

"I'm sorry, Marcia. I really am listening." After ushering her through the doorway, Blake walked over to the bar and poured two glasses of wine, handing one of them to her.

"It isn't important. But something is bothering

you. I noticed it all evening. I don't believe you were aware of anything that went on." She touched his cheek. "You've been keeping a horrendous pace lately. When will you be able to relax and enjoy life?"

Relax and enjoy life. How many times had his father and Scott said that to him? How did they expect him to relax and enjoy life when they had done everything in their power to mess it up?

He shook his head. "I'm sorry, Marcia. I've been terrible company tonight."

She placed her wineglass on a small table by the sofa and wrapped her arms around his neck. "I'm always willing to allow you to make it up to me, you know," she whispered, kissing him.

Blake had never before noticed how tall Marcia was. In her heels she was only a few inches shorter than he, whereas Angel had to stand on her toes to kiss him and he still had to bend over her to—

What the hell was he thinking of? He had a beautiful woman in his arms, kissing him passionately, and all he could think about was Angel.

I must be losing my mind.

Marcia pulled away from him with a slight frown. "Darling, what's wrong?"

Blake took the opportunity to pick up his drink and walk over to the plate-glass window that gave an aerial view of downtown San Francisco and the bay area. "There's something I have to tell you, Marcia."

She followed him to the window after picking up her drink. "You sound so serious. Has something happened I don't know about?"

"Yes, and I'm having trouble finding a way to tell you."

"Your father left you nothing but debts and you want to marry me for my money, is that it?" Her husky voice held a slight tremor of laughter. "But, darling, this is so sudden!"

Funny that she should choose tonight to bring up the subject of marriage.

"Do you remember my mentioning Angel Bennington to you?"

She paused, thinking a moment. "Oh, yes. Your fathers were partners in the business."

"That's right."

"I'm sure their estates are closely tied in with the business. Is she your partner in the company now?" she asked with casual interest.

"No. The business was left to me." *Under certain stipulations.* "However, she's receiving compensation." *Of sorts.*

"I see." Marcia sat down on the sofa and sipped from her glass once more.

"No, you don't see because I'm not explaining this well." He ran his hand through his hair with agitation. "Angel and I have been spending a considerable amount of time together during the past few weeks." Blake caught himself pacing, a bad habit of his when he was disturbed. He forced himself to sit down next to Marcia. He took a large swallow of wine, then set the glass down with quiet deliberation.

"The thing is, Marcia, I've asked Angel to marry me."

"*Marry* you!" She stared at him in disbelief.

The silence in the room was so intense that Blake suddenly became aware of the quiet ticking of the chime clock in the other room.

"Yes."

"But I don't understand. You've always given everyone the impression you never intended to marry."

"I wasn't aware of that."

"Well, you have. Why do you suppose I've been content with the relationship we have? It's more than you've ever had with another woman. It took me almost three years to get your attention, three long years of being at the right place at the right time so that you would even *notice* me." Marcia jumped from her chair and strode to the windows overlooking downtown San Francisco.

"I never knew, Marcia." He got up and followed her to the window. "I never meant to hurt you. I wasn't aware of your feelings."

"Of course you weren't. I'm not that obvious." Marcia continued to stare blindly out the window.

After a moment she spoke in a low voice. "I have tried to be everything you wanted me to be, Blake. You don't like possessive women...I'm not possessive. You don't like jealousy...I have fought every jealous urge I've ever had around you. And now you calmly announce to me that you are going to marry someone else. What do you expect me to say, Blake? 'Gee, that's swell'?" She spun around and faced him, her green eyes glistening. "Tell me something...if you will. Did you ever once consider asking *me* to marry you?"

Blake saw the pain in her eyes and mentally kicked himself for his blindness. He had accepted Marcia in his life without question. She had always appeared calm, serene, cool and collected. He had never given their relationship much thought until recently. Marcia had always been there for him whenever he called, whenever he needed someone to talk to, and he never wondered why she was willing to wait to see him whenever he had time for her.

And now you've managed to hurt her, you stupid ass, he told himself.

It wouldn't help matters to tell her the truth about his marriage to Angel. He had been a louse to Marcia, even though he hadn't really faced it until now. What was the point in explaining that he was marrying another woman for business reasons? Blake was seeing himself from another person's point of view and he didn't like what he saw. Not at all.

"Marcia, I'm sorry I've hurt you. That was never my intention. This thing with Angel and I just happened. I had no idea you thought of me as more than a friend."

Marcia gave a quick shake of her head. Blake wasn't sure if she were trying to clear her thoughts or to deny his statement. Perhaps the gesture was a little of both. He watched as she made a conscious effort to gain control of her emotions. She walked over to her drink and picked up her glass.

Blake couldn't remember a time when he had felt so helpless. How the hell had he gotten into such a predicament, anyway? None of this was Marcia's fault. She was just as much a victim of the circumstances as he or Angel.

Marcia started to speak and her voice broke. She cleared her throat and slowly raised her eyes until she met his gaze.

"When are you getting married?"

"In May."

"I see." Carefully placing her glass back on the table, Marcia picked up her coat. "Then there's really no more to be said, is there?"

Blake took the coat from her and held it so she could slip it on. They made the drive to her home in silence. He walked her to the door and stopped. "If it's any consolation to you, I recognize what a bastard I've been to you."

Marcia resolutely met his gaze. "Actually, it's no

consolation whatsoever." She gave a slight shrug. "I gambled on being the woman in your life if and when you ever decided to marry. I lost." She turned away from him and opened the door. "I hope she's what you want," he heard her say in a muffled tone. She closed the door behind her.

Blake lay in bed that night for hours, staring up at the darkened ceiling. Marcia deserved better treatment than she had received from him. He wondered how he could have been so unaware of her true feelings. Sometime during the early morning hours he had to face the fact that he was no longer certain of anything in his life.

Harry insisted on hosting the engagement party honoring the children of his two closest friends. Blake obligingly left the details in Harry's capable hands and devoted himself, with a certain amount of unconscious relief, to the familiar and soothing world of cutthroat corporate maneuvering.

Angel, meanwhile, was faced with her success in the art world and her insistence on anonymity. Michelle had forwarded her mail, and on the Thursday before the engagement party Angel discovered a letter from a gallery in San Francisco that wanted to have a showing of AB's paintings. Her agent had filled her in on the details and suggested, since she was already there, that she might find it agreeable.

She couldn't possibly. There were not enough

available paintings unless she spent the next several months totally devoted to her work. Sinking down into the comfortable chair in front of the library fireplace, Angel realized what she was telling herself. Her career was already being shoved to the background to make way for her marriage.

"No!" She glanced around, embarrassed at the realization that she was talking out loud. What was she thinking of? Of course she would have the showing, regardless of the effort it took for her to prepare. Blake certainly wasn't letting his intended relationship with her interfere with his life.

Angel scanned her agent's letter once again. They were proposing a June showing. That would give her almost five months. She had a couple of paintings that were nearing completion here, more in Paris. If she left next week and worked eighteen-hour days she just might be able to do it. If not, she might be able to borrow some of her paintings that had already been sold.

The clock on the mantel chimed softly and Angel remembered she had intended to go shopping for a dress for Saturday night. "What a waste of time," she muttered, forcing herself to go upstairs and change clothes. She hated to shop when she needed something. It was much more fun to wander around and look at everything at a leisurely pace. But it couldn't be helped. Too bad Michelle and Suzanne weren't there to offer their advice.

Several hours later Angel had just about given up in despair. Because of her small size she had to watch ruthlessly that a dress didn't overpower her. She preferred simple, classic lines and vibrant colors and was having a devil of a time trying to find something.

When she saw the shimmering white gown, Angel knew her search was over. Its iridescence emphasized the superb cut and style and when she tried it on, she smiled brilliantly. The bodice lovingly cupped her trim figure and emphasized the tininess of her waist, and the sleek lines faithfully followed her gently curving hips and thighs, flaring ever so slightly at her ankles. It clung so well there was no likelihood that she would be able to wear much underneath it.

Angel shrugged. So what? Blake would be the only one who might object and since his mind was on much loftier matters, such as how to do in a competitor and place a stranglehold on some corporation, she was certain he wouldn't care.

Blake did not see the full effect of Angel's gown until they arrived at the ballroom of the hotel. He helped her off with her floor-length satin cape and when she turned around he caught his breath. Her dress seemed to drape across her breasts, their rounded fullness apparently the only thing keeping the neckline from falling to her waist. The rest of the dress looked as though it had been sewn on her, the soft white changing subtly into colors every time she breathed.

"Angel, my dear, you look absolutely stunning," Harry said coming up behind them wearing a huge grin. "Doesn't she, Blake?"

"Stunning," he muttered half under his breath. "Did you bring that dress from Paris?"

She looked up at him in surprise. "Why, no. You told me to find something suitable here in San Francisco."

"You look very young and virginal, I must say," Harry enthused. "Just what you'd expect of a newly engaged young lady."

If that dress was Harry's idea of a virginal gown, it was no wonder he had never married. He knew nothing about women, Blake decided. The problem with it was that it gave a deceptive appearance. It was almost as though you could see through to her skin glowing underneath it. Perhaps that was because Angel had the true redhead's translucent complexion and skin tones.

Her hair hung loose around her shoulders, dipping and swirling around them, and her eyes sparkled with excitement. "I can't remember when I've looked forward to anything the way I have to this party, Harry. Somehow it brings Papa closer to me—to be able to meet his friends again after all these years. He had so many of them."

"Yes, he did. They all loved him and I know will

be pleased to hear you intend to live over here now so that they can become better acquainted with you.''

She glanced up at Blake from under her lowered lashes. He looked positively grim. Was he bored already? The party hadn't even started.

Harry glanced around the room with satisfaction. "I'm really pleased with the way everything looks. Todd and Scott would be proud to be here with us tonight." He took Angel's hand. "Why don't we go over by the door and be prepared to meet people as they come in?" Taking her acquiescence for granted, he tucked her small hand into the bend of his elbow and escorted her across the room, leaving Blake to follow.

Blake had a feeling it was going to be a very long evening. He watched the soft material of Angel's dress slide and shift across her delicately curved derriere and felt his body responding to the view. A very long evening.

Almost an hour later the room was filled with laughing people enjoying themselves, everyone eager to get to know Blake's chosen wife better. Blake and Angel were just leaving the receiving line when Blake's best friend arrived.

"It's about time, Jeremy. I thought you decided to forgo the pleasure of our company this evening."

"Not on your life," the good-looking blond man replied with a devilish grin. "The day Blake Carlyle introduces us to his soon-to-be-bride is the day I break all speed records getting back from L.A. to make it." He stared expectantly at Angel.

Blake kept his arm around her waist. "Angel, I want you to meet the fellow whom I've spent a lifetime trying to keep out of trouble, starting back in our preschool days. This is Jeremy Jordan, the Fourth."

Angel took Jeremy's hand and smiled. "The Fourth?"

"Yes. Isn't that a rotten thing to do to a kid? I've already promised the family that the numbers stop right here."

Angel tilted her head slightly and said, "Oh, that's too bad. I'm sure you would make an excellent husband and father." She felt Blake stiffen.

"Oh, I fully intend to marry someday...and even have children. But none of them will be called Jeremy. It isn't all that great a name, anyway."

"I wouldn't say that. I like it."

Jeremy glanced at his friend and recognized the scowl that was forming across his brow. Recognized it—and ignored it. "Are you sure you want to marry this guy, Angel? Wouldn't you prefer a more lighthearted, fun-loving companion? I'd be more than willing to make an offer if I thought I could win you away from him."

Angel laughed delightedly. Jeremy was just what she needed after the past few dismal weeks. His blue eyes twinkled with mischief and she knew he was aware that his remarks were not being accepted by Blake with any degree of good humor. She shook her head, wearing a mock-sorrowful expression on her face.

"I'm so sorry, Jeremy, but you see, I was promised to Blake from the cradle. Our families brought us up to think only of each other as a mate. I couldn't break such a lifelong tradition, now, could I?"

Blake stared at her in dismay. Did she intend to admit the truth of their marriage to Jeremy? She had come damned close with her silly story. What the hell was she trying to pull?

Jeremy bowed before her. "Then if you will not honor me with your hand in marriage, how about a dance, milady?"

Angel glanced around and realized all the other guests were helping themselves to the buffet or dancing to the tunes provided by the musicians at the end of the room.

"I'd love to, Jeremy. Thank you so much for asking." She smiled innocently at Blake. "If you'll excuse us..."

Blake stared at his fiancée and his former best friend inimically as they walked away from him, then forced himself to look relaxed and headed for the bar.

Harry had watched the unfolding scene from a safe distance and was delighted to see that Blake was not having things all his own way. He needed to learn flexibility, and Harry had a hunch Angel was going to be just the person to teach him.

No one could deny that Angel was an overwhelming success that evening. Blake's friends were enchanted, if somewhat startled, by his choice of wife. Blake had always been known as quiet, solemn and serious. He and Marcia had appeared to be a well-matched pair. But they could certainly understand Angel's stealing his heart.

She was like a pixie—a person was almost afraid to blink in her presence for fear she might disappear. Her tinkling laugh caused heads to turn with amusement and enjoyment of her lighthearted responses. All who attended the party found themselves basking in the glow of her warm personality.

All except Blake. Jeremy found him standing near the bar watching the crowd surrounding Angel, while she tried to decide which one she had agreed to dance with next. Jeremy noted the slight frown on his friend's face and grinned. He knew quite well that Blake wasn't used to the emotions that Angel appeared to be creating within him. Jeremy wondered what Blake intended to do about those feelings.

"I believe your choice of bride is a smash hit with all your friends, old buddy."

Blake glanced around, unaware until he spoke that Jeremy had joined him. He had been concentrating on Angel. Lifting his drink to his lips, he took another swallow. "So it would seem."

"Have you danced with her yet?"

"I didn't want to fight the mob."

Jeremy laughed. "Don't tell me you're jealous of the attention she's getting!"

"No. I just wish she didn't look quite so flashy."

"Flashy. Angel? Surely you jest. Her gown is in the greatest of good taste. It goes very well with her coloring."

Blake watched as Angel did an energetic fast dance with a fellow Blake had always considered a good friend—until now. At the moment he felt a sincere need to place his fist in the middle of the man's face and drag Angel off the dance floor. He still wasn't certain how she'd managed to keep her neckline in place all evening.

He took another sip of his drink.

"I don't suppose Marcia took the news of your engagement well. I haven't had a chance to talk with you since you dropped the bombshell of a surprise engagement on all of us."

"No, she didn't. Since she's the only woman I've been seeing, it was natural that she might expect me to marry her if I ever married anyone." Blake felt very uncomfortable every time he was reminded of Marcia.

Jeremy nodded. "That was a common supposition for all of us. But now that I've had a chance to meet Angel I can certainly see why you snapped her up before any of us got the chance to grab her. Actually,

I never before realized what exquisite taste you have, Blake. I'm impressed."

Blake said nothing. Instead, he continued to watch as Angel began dancing a slow number with another one of his ex-friends. He had never realized how Randy pawed his dancing partners before, and if he didn't keep his hands where they belonged, Blake was going to remove one of them for him—at the wrist.

Jeremy waved his hand in front of Blake's face. "You still there, Blake?"

Blake glanced around. "What?"

"Oh, nothing. Just trying to make conversation. You've really got it bad, haven't you?"

"I have no idea what you're talking about."

Jeremy studied his friend for several moments, then smiled delightedly. "You know, I believe you. Hell, this situation gets funnier by the minute." He grabbed a glass of champagne from the tray of a passing waiter. "Here, Blake. What you need is another drink."

Blake stared at the glass in Jeremy's hand. "No, thanks. I'll see you later," he muttered, and strode toward the dance floor with a grim determination that caused Jeremy to burst into laughter.

Angel had enjoyed herself all evening but had seen very little of Blake. He seemed content to stand around visiting with their guests. He must not enjoy dancing, one of her favorite forms of entertainment.

She glanced up at the man dancing with her and smiled. What was his name? Randy? Ralph? She'd lost track and it really didn't matter.

When the music ended Angel turned around and found Blake standing directly in front of her. "I believe it's my turn, isn't it?" he asked in a husky tone that caused a trembling to start deep inside of her. The orchestra was playing a medley of love songs and she glided into his arms, tilting her head back to look up at him.

"I didn't think you liked to dance," she murmured.

"Whatever gave you that idea?"

"My first clue was the fact that the band has been playing for two hours and this is the first time you've danced."

"You noticed."

"Of course."

"I decided to be patient and wait my turn. Now the others will have to learn patience." He pulled her even closer so that their bodies fitted closely together. She flowed against him, relaxing and letting the music fill her mind and senses.

They spent the rest of the evening together and no one even attempted to separate them. Blake's friends were amused at his possessiveness, a new trait they had never before witnessed. It seemed to be so out of character. He certainly had some hidden dimensions that had only recently become apparent to those around him.

The clock was softly chiming two o'clock when Blake and Angel returned to her home and entered the library. A soft fire still flickered in the fireplace, and the room felt warm and cozy.

"Would you like some coffee before you leave?" Angel asked, sinking down on the comfortable love seat in front of the fire and slipping off her shoes.

Blake sat down next to her, pulling her small feet into his lap and massaging them. "Not really."

"Oh, that feels good. I can't remember having danced so much in one evening."

"I would have guessed you made a habit of going out when you lived in Paris."

"Not really. We spent more time talking and arguing the merits of different well-known artists than we spent out dancing."

His hand slid up her leg and began to knead the muscle in her calf. "You take your art very seriously, don't you?"

Angel slowly relaxed as his fingers worked their magic. "Yes, I do."

"I wouldn't want you to give it up just because you'll be moving here to the States."

"Oh, I would never do that. Painting is too much a part of me. It's like breathing and eating—a necessary part of my existence."

He gently lifted her, settling her on his lap.

"Would you show me some of your work sometime?" His mouth found the soft tender spot just beneath her ear, his breath causing a chill to race down her spine.

She nodded, trying to find her voice. "If you want to see it."

His lips moved across her delicately tinted cheek. "I do. Very much."

Her warm scent filled his senses and Blake tilted her face up to his so that his lips found hers. The kiss set off tiny electrical shocks throughout his system and he pulled her closer, feeling the rapid beat of her heart against his chest.

The fine material of her dress was no barrier and Blake no longer resisted the temptation to place his hand along the provocative line of cloth that draped her breasts. Her breath was coming in short pants and he recognized that she was as disturbed by their closeness as he was.

His hand slid underneath the material, confirming what he had suspected all evening. She wore nothing else. Cupping her firm breast in his large hand he stroked its smooth surface, feeling the nipple contract into a hard knot beneath his fingertips.

Angel moaned softly, giving Blake the opportunity to deepen the kiss even further, his tongue darting into the slight opening of her sweetly swollen lips. She tasted so good. He couldn't seem to get enough of her.

Blake ran his other hand along her leg, feeling the slight tremor of her body and the chills that he seemed to be provoking wherever he touched her. He wanted her. He couldn't remember ever having wanted someone so much.

But not tonight, you idiot. Not tonight. What sort of Neanderthal will she think you are? You've made it clear the marriage is one of convenience and you can't even keep your hands off her until the wedding!

Blake slackened his hold and stared down at her with a sense of confusion that bordered on fear. What was happening to him? Was she some sort of witch that had cast a spell on him? Some "angel"! She was the most unheavenly angel he could ever hope to meet.

He pulled her head down so that she snuggled her face into his neck and they sat there together, trying to get their breath. Blake lost track of time. It felt so good just to sit there and hold her in his arms. He didn't think he could ever become bored holding her.

"Are you still leaving on Tuesday?" he finally asked in a low voice.

"Yes."

"Do you want me to take you to the airport?"

"No."

"How about having dinner with me Monday night?"

She nodded, still too shaken over what had occurred between the two of them to be able to speak.

Blake stood up, allowing her to slide slowly down the length of his body. She could feel the rush of heat to her face when she felt his obvious arousal. Angel wasn't used to being in such close contact with a man. Jean-Pierre was the only other man besides her father she had been around and he treated her like a kid sister. Blake, on the other hand, treated her as though she were an experienced woman. Surely there must be some middle ground in there somewhere.

"I'll pick you up on Monday at seven, all right?" he asked.

She nodded.

He bent over and kissed her softly on the mouth. She looked like a sleepy little girl, her hair mussed from his fingers, her eyelids half-closed. "Good night, Angel."

"Good night." Her hand trailed down the side of his cheek in a fond gesture of which she was unaware. He smiled.

"I'll see you Monday."

Chapter Five

As it turned out Blake did see Angel on Monday, but not exactly when and where he expected.

Jeremy met him for lunch and they went to one of the better-known restaurants high above the streets of San Francisco. Blake was trying to catch Jeremy up on the recent events in his life when he noticed that Jeremy was no longer listening to him. Instead, he was staring past him with a look of surprised concern.

"What's the matter?" Blake asked, glancing around.

Jeremy's gaze darted back to his friend with dismay. "Oh, nothing. Thought I recognized someone for a moment, but there was only a superficial likeness."

Unfortunately for Jeremy's attempt to dissemble, the maître d' was leading Angel and her unknown escort to a table near the front of the room, placing them by a window.

Blake froze when he recognized her, although she looked considerably different than he had ever seen her. She wore a severely tailored navy suit with a powder-blue ruffled blouse. Her hair was elegantly fashioned in a chignon, giving her a stately, sophisticated image that was hard to reconcile to the sleepy, seductive woman he had held in his arms only a few nights before.

Blake's narrowed gaze focused on the man seated across from Angel, his rapt attention to his companion causing Blake's knuckles to turn white as he clenched his hands.

"Who is he?" Jeremy asked quietly.

"I have no idea."

"I didn't know she knew anyone in San Francisco other than mutual friends and business associates of yours."

"Neither did I."

"I'm sure there's a perfectly satisfactory explanation, Blake. You don't need to look as though you intend to do him in over his luncheon special."

Blake's gaze returned to Jeremy's. "I'm not upset with him. Why should I be? I don't even know the poor sucker. I'm just amazed that I was so taken in by that damned air of innocence Angel projects with such style." He picked up his cup and drained it. "Are you ready to go?"

Jeremy glanced back at the other couple. "Shouldn't we stop by and say hello? I don't think she's even seen us."

"I have no intention of walking over there as though expecting to be introduced. What Angel does with her time is her business. She owes me no explanations."

Jeremy followed him out of the large restaurant, shaking his head. Blake was in worse shape than he thought. Good old logical, objective Blake was acting like a jealous, lovesick fool. *Welcome to the world of human frailties, my friend,* he silently offered.

Angel was concentrating on what Mr. Huntington, the owner of the gallery, was saying when she happened to glance up and see Blake and Jeremy leaving the restaurant. *Oh, no, what are they doing here, of all places?* she wondered frantically. She forced her gaze back to the distinguished man before her.

"I can't tell you what a pleasure it is to finally meet you, Ms. Bennington. I'm sure you're aware that no one had any idea that AB was in fact a woman. Your work has such a boldness of style, such a classic simplicity, almost a starkness that is usually associated with the more masculine artist."

"Which is exactly why I didn't want to be judged

by my gender," she said quietly. "My art has always stood on its own and I don't want that changed."

"I can certainly appreciate that, and I want you to know how honored I am that you have divulged your identity to me. Let me assure you that I will not betray that confidence." His long, narrow face registered his sincerity, and Angel nodded.

"My agent told me that you could be trusted. I trust my agent's judgment. Therefore—" she shrugged "—I thought it would make it more simple to plan my show with you directly, rather than through my agent, especially since I will be moving to San Francisco in a few months."

Mr. Huntington permitted himself a small smile of satisfaction. "The loss to the European art circles will certainly be our gain, Ms. Bennington. I feel certain you will enjoy our marvelous city. It has so much to offer."

They made plans through their lunch and Angel could only give fleeting thought to Blake. Had he seen her? If so, why hadn't he come by the table? If not, should she mention that she was there?

The problem was that she did not want him to know about her showing. Angel wasn't ready to tell Blake who she was. It hardly mattered in his world, anyway.

It was almost three o'clock before Angel and Mr. Huntington parted company. He seemed to be bubbling with anticipation for the upcoming show and she only hoped he wouldn't be disappointed with the number of paintings she could make available.

By the time she got home it was too late to work in her studio and she decided to take a nap, hoping to decide what to tell Blake when she saw him.

As it turned out, she had no need to tell him anything. From his casual manner and conversation, Angel decided he must not have seen her. Therefore, she could think of no good reason to bring up her meeting with Mr. Huntington herself. She soothed her conscience by deciding that eventually she would tell him about her recognized status in the art world, but not just yet.

Blake took her to a restaurant she had never seen and they had a delicious meal. Making a conscious effort to learn more about his world, Angel plied him with intelligent questions about the corporation and what he was accomplishing, so that by the time the meal was over she had gained a great deal of insight into the tremendous responsibilities Blake had shouldered when their fathers were killed.

The musicians were getting ready to begin playing when Angel glanced up and saw a distinguished-looking older man threading his way through the tables, leading a reluctant-looking young woman who was tall, dark headed and extremely attractive. She glanced at Blake and saw his relaxed smile fade and his impassive mask appear.

"Blake! I thought that was you, sitting over here

in this dark corner," the man said with an inquiring smile. He looked at Angel with obvious surprise, and a slight frown formed on his face. "I was just asking Marcia the other day why we haven't seen much of you lately."

Angel looked up at the woman and almost winced. So this was Marcia. She had a natural serenity about her that was very becoming. Her black hair shone in the soft light of the restaurant and her skin looked like alabaster. After one glance at Angel, she had dropped her eyes, refusing to look at either of them.

Blake stood up and offered his hand to the other man. "It's good to see you again, Richard. Angel, I want you to meet Marcia and Richard Sinclair. This is Angel Bennington, my fiancée."

"Your fiancée!" Richard repeated in a shocked tone. He quickly recovered and with slightly heightened color in his cheeks attempted to smile at Angel. "I'm so very pleased to meet you, Miss Bennington. Are you by any chance Scott Bennington's daughter?"

"Yes, I am."

"Would you care to join us?" Blake asked in a polite voice.

Marcia was shaking her head when Richard said, "If you don't mind, Blake. I wanted to ask you about a couple of things I heard about the market."

"Certainly." Blake signaled the waiter for two more chairs. Because the table was small, Angel was forced to crowd her chair next to Blake's. No sooner had she moved next to him than he draped his arm around her shoulder, pulling her close to his side.

Richard looked at his drink, brought by the efficient waiter, the way a man lost in the desert for days might eye water, and Angel realized he wasn't as relaxed as he wanted them to think. Then why had he joined them? She glanced back at Marcia and smiled. "I'm so glad to meet you, Marcia. Blake has mentioned you several times."

Blake suddenly reached for his drink and she wondered about the atmosphere of the restaurant that caused so many of the men to develop unquenchable thirsts.

"Oh, has he?" Marcia watched the expression on Blake's face. "I find that rather surprising, under the circumstances."

"Oh, surely not," Angel exclaimed. "Blake has mentioned how much he wants me to get to know all of his friends. Are you involved with the business world?"

Richard laughed. "The only part of the business world my daughter is involved in is spending the assets as soon as she can get her hands on them!"

"Father!"

Angel smiled at both of them with sympathetic understanding. "Spoken like a true father. They just don't understand us, do they, Marcia? What earthly good is having money if you don't enjoy it, I always say."

"Funny, I never heard you say that," Blake whispered in her ear in an undertone.

She ignored him.

Marcia took in with dismay the intimate pose of the couple seated across from her. Blake was not an affectionate person and could be depended upon to show discretion in a public place. Yet here he sat with his fiancée and if they were any closer she would be in his lap! How had Angel managed to breach all of his barriers?

"I understand that you paint, is that correct?" Marcia asked in an attempt to keep the conversation going.

"Yes."

"It's really a wonderful hobby, isn't it? So relaxing. I'm sure your father must have been very proud of your talent."

"He was."

"And now Blake can take up where your father left off, continuing to encourage you and look after you, just as your father would have wanted."

Blake made a slight choking sound and Angel forced herself to turn her head, causing her face to brush against his cheek. She pulled back slightly, forcing herself to show concern. "Are you all right?"

"Couldn't be better. Thoughtful of you to ask.

Care for another drink?" His urbane manner created within Angel a sudden urge to slap him.

"No, thank you."

"Have you set a date for the wedding?" Richard asked, trying to keep the rather heavy conversation going.

"In May, more than likely. Angel is returning to France tomorrow. She needed some time to conclude her affairs over there." *Oh, Lord, what a poor choice of words!* he realized as soon as he said them.

Richard's laughter floated around the table. "I can certainly understand that. I'm sure you have a few loose ends to tie up, as well, don't you? I mean, before you settle down into a staid married existence?" His eyes glinted as he glanced from Blake to his daughter.

Angel watched the color flood Marcia's cheeks. Her father appeared to have no sensitivity where his daughter's feelings were concerned. Whatever he had intended to discuss could better be said some other time.

Angel dropped her hand nonchalantly on Blake's thigh and gently squeezed, gaining his immediate and undivided attention. "I'm a little tired, Blake. Would it be too much trouble to take me home?"

He would never recognize the sacrifice. Angel had already become entranced with the music and had been hoping they would be able to dance, but it was more important for everyone's sake to bring this scene to a close.

Blake acknowledged her suggestion with alacrity. He was on his feet in seconds, drawing out her chair and excusing them from the Sinclairs.

Blake was quiet on the way home and Angel couldn't help but wonder how he had felt about suddenly seeing Marcia again. She knew better than to ask. He had made it clear his relationship with Marcia was none of her business.

"I'm sorry about tonight," he finally said in a low voice.

"You don't owe me an apology," she responded quietly.

"Marcia obviously hadn't told her father about our engagement."

"Then she already knew about it?"

He looked at her in surprise. "Of course. I wouldn't have wanted her to find out from someone else."

Angel heard the regret in his voice and felt as though a cold hand had squeezed her heart.

"I was very much aware of how you got us out of there tonight," he went on to say. "I don't know why everyone seems to think you need protecting from the world. You can hold your own in any situation."

Angel recalled the night of their engagement party

and the way she had melted into his arms on the sofa. "Not every situation," she murmured.

"Would you mind if I call you while you are in France?" he asked, effectively changing the subject.

She glanced around in surprise. "I would like that."

"Good." He pulled up in front of her door, got out of the car, helped her out and opened the front door for her. But he didn't follow her in. "I won't keep you up tonight. You need your rest. I'll see you in about four months, then, is that right?"

She nodded, suddenly bereft at the thought of leaving him.

"You won't change your mind?"

"I gave you my word, Blake."

Her quiet assurance that her word was all he needed made him wince. His usual control deserted him and he stepped forward into the house, closing the door behind him. Then leaning against it he pulled her into him, her body draped across the hard muscled length of him. "Don't forget me, Angel," he muttered before his mouth found hers.

His sudden move had caught her off guard and she was in his arms and pulled off her feet before she knew what was happening. But when his lips found hers with a passionate intensity, Angel recognized she was exactly where she wanted to be, wrapped securely in Blake's arms.

* * *

Paris had lost its charm for Angel. If she hadn't been so busy she might have ended up moping, but there was no hope for that. She spent every possible minute at her easel.

Angel was surprised to discover that she missed Blake, but no more surprised than her roommates were to discover she had agreed to marry an American.

"You? Get married? You cannot be serious!" Suzanne exclaimed.

"Oh, but I am, Suzanne. Very serious."

Michelle shook her head. "It is because you have lost your father. But there is no substitute for a father's love, Angel. Surely you must know that."

"Believe me, Michelle, Blake Carlyle is absolutely nothing like my father."

"But, *chérie,* have you given the matter proper consideration?" Suzanne questioned gently. "How can you know this is what you want? You just met the man."

"I know."

"And you've made it clear to everyone who knows you that you never intended to marry," Michelle added.

"I know."

The two Frenchwomen looked at each other and shrugged.

"Is that all you can say?" Michelle finally asked. "'I know'?"

"I really think I'm in love," she finally admitted.

"You *think*! Well, for God's sake, don't decide to marry this man until you know for sure!" Michelle insisted.

"All I can say is I'm glad you had the sense to come home for a few months to think it over," Suzanne added.

Angel shook her head. "That isn't why I came back. The wedding date is set. We are definitely getting married. But in addition, I'm going to have a showing in San Francisco in June and I want to get as many paintings prepared as possible before I go back."

"Is there nothing we can say to make you change your mind?"

She smiled. "No. But thank you both for caring. If you were to meet him, perhaps you'd understand." But she doubted it. Blake was so different from any other man she'd ever known. Suzanne and Michelle would not understand the fascination. And how could they? She could scarcely understand it herself.

Blake arrived at the San Francisco airport almost an hour early but he had been too restless to stay at the office. He had talked with Angel several times over the past several weeks. He had gotten into the habit of sharing his days with her and insisting on hearing about hers. There were times he could barely hear her for the noise and she explained that her roommates had company. She had told him that she was staying busy painting and he believed her. But he was afraid to ask how her friends had taken the news that she was moving away. He particularly didn't want to know about her male friends' reaction.

Blake had determinedly put out of his mind all thought of the other men in her life. It didn't matter what she had done. He recognized that once she had made the commitment to marry him she would be loyal to him. He knew that because he recognized more and more each day how very much like her father Angel truly was.

Not long after Angel had left, Blake had gone over to his father's home and tried to picture her living there. He couldn't. Dark, heavy drapes had covered all the windows, and the massive mahogany furniture had towered in every room. The somber colors had been depressing and he'd known that something would have to be done.

All of that was gone now. In their place were golden tones, sheer drapes and modern, comfortable furniture. He hoped she approved and had a sudden sense of hesitancy. Perhaps he should have waited for her to do the decorating.

Oh, well, if she didn't like it, she could always have it done over.

Angel's flight was announced over the loudspeaker and Blake stood up, realizing that he had been lost in his thoughts for almost an hour. He felt his heartbeat quicken. She was here. He would be seeing her in just a few minutes. And in less than two weeks, they would be married. Blake no longer thought about the original reasons for their marriage.

He stood back from the entrance where those coming off the international flight would be deplaning. The plane had been one of the larger ones and a crowd of people seemed to be surging through the door.

And then he saw her, her bright head shining in the sea of nameless faces. He started moving toward her, his heartbeat increasing with every step he took. He was only a few feet away from her when he noticed the man with his arm tucked in hers, talking rapidly and expansively. She was looking up at him, laughing at whatever he was saying.

Just before they reached him, Blake took in the man's brown curly hair, broad shoulders and casual dress.

Angel glanced up. "Blake! I didn't know you were going to meet my plane. How wonderful!" She threw herself into his arms and kissed him exuberantly. Then she grabbed his arm and turned to the curly-headed man watching them in amusement. "Jean-Pierre—this is Blake Carlyle. Blake, I want you to meet Jean-Pierre Armand, who insisted on coming over with me. He said he wanted to meet the man who finally convinced me to marry him."

Chapter Six

Blake numbly shook the hand of the man before him. In heavily accented English, Jean-Pierre said, "I am so very pleased to meet you, Monsieur Carlyle. Angel has told us so much about you."

She laughed. "I believe Suzanne and Michelle were delighted to pack me up and get me out of there. I was getting very boring, I'm sure."

The Frenchman looked down at her with obvious affection. "Never that, *chérie,* that would be impossible."

"Of course you must say that, Jean-Pierre. Otherwise you might not have a place to stay!"

Blake stared at the two of them in bewilderment. When Angel noticed his expression she explained. "Since Jean-Pierre spent most of his money for his plane ticket, I told him he could stay with me. There are several people here who would make excellent contacts for him. Since he was so concerned about me, I suggested he come along and meet you, and I would introduce him to some of the people I have met here who could greatly help his career."

"He's going to stay with you?" Blake repeated slowly.

Angel looked at him with a slight smile. "And why not? With five bedrooms and even more baths, I doubt that we're going to be crowded."

"I see." His mind was whirling. He hadn't expected this. Of course Angel had not expected him to be at the airport, either. He wondered if she would have even mentioned Jean-Pierre's presence at her home.

She took each of the men by the elbow and began to shepherd them down the concourse to the baggage-claim area.

"So you intend to live with Jean-Pierre until we get married?" Blake asked carefully.

Was it possible that Blake was jealous? The thought boosted Angel's spirits considerably. She had tried not to think about the evenings he might have spent with Marcia during the past few months. It wouldn't hurt him to discover how it felt to be a little uncertain of someone.

"Why not?" she asked blandly.

Jean-Pierre began to laugh. "Ah, Angel, don't you

understand? Your fiancé thinks that you and I are sleeping together." He looked over her head at Blake. "Isn't that so?"

"The thought had crossed my mind," Blake admitted sardonically.

Angel had forgotten that Blake was convinced she had a legion of lovers. She thought he had gotten to know her better than that. Obviously that was not the case.

"Oh, that's right. We did discuss this earlier, didn't we? Well, you mustn't worry. I explained to Jean-Pierre your fear that our firstborn might not be yours, and he magnanimously agreed to refrain from making love to me when I returned to Paris." She gave Blake her most winsome smile. "Jean-Pierre was *most* accommodating and agreed not to touch me!"

"Angel, you little monster!" Jean-Pierre was chuckling and shaking his head. "What sort of nonsense are you telling the poor man?"

"Exactly what he expected to hear."

"Hardly," Blake admitted. He stepped back to allow Angel to go ahead of him through the gate to the baggage-claim area.

"I have known Angel since she was practically an infant, which she still is in many ways," Jean-Pierre explained patiently. "I became her self-appointed guardian when she first arrived at school and it has become an ingrained habit with me, I'm afraid. However, I am more than willing to allow you the privilege, Monsieur Carlyle. I have great sympathy for you. You show a great deal of courage in undertaking the task of looking after Angel."

"Nonsense. I don't need anyone to look after me."

The men steadily met each other's gaze, and each recognized a common bond in the other. As though they had just that moment met, Blake suddenly stuck his hand out once again. "Please call me Blake."

Jean-Pierre nodded with Gallic dignity. "Thank you. You must, of course, call me Jean-Pierre."

"Oh, that bag is mine," Angel interrupted to point out. "Can you get it before it disappears again?"

Blake still didn't like the idea of Jean-Pierre's staying with Angel but he knew better than to try to veto the plan. Angel's independence was one of her most endearing traits. Usually. At other times he was beginning to realize it would be a real pain.

The day of the wedding between Blake Carlyle and Angel Bennington was typical for San Francisco. The fog didn't burn off until almost noon, but by midafternoon the sun glinted off the water of the bay and brought a sense of hope for the future to Angel.

Harry picked her up and drove her to the small church where she was to meet Blake and Jeremy. Jean-Pierre had refused her invitation to be present, explaining that a private wedding was just that and, besides, he needed to finish working on the sculpture he had started. Because her studio was so large they had both had plenty of room to work together, something they were used to, and they had spent many hours in pleasant silence together.

Angel stared out the window of the car at the other homes in her neighborhood and wished she didn't feel so nervous. She felt so inadequate to the occasion. What did she know about marriage? Her parents' disastrous union had certainly been less than a good example.

During the recent weeks of preparing for her art show she had tried not to think about the permanent commitment she was making. Now that was all she could think about.

Angel knew that she would never have agreed to marry Blake if she hadn't been more than halfway in love with him, but the very thought of loving him, and being vulnerable where he was concerned, frightened her.

She had needed her time away from him to come to terms objectively with what she was doing and why. Angel respected her father's judgment and if he thought their marriage would work, she had to try.

Harry reached over and patted her clasped hands. "This will all work out just fine, Angel. Wait and see."

"I hope so," she murmured.

"I think Blake will make you a fine husband. He's got a great deal of character and integrity, you know. He'll honor the commitment he's making today."

Angel studied the man driving the car. Harry had aged considerably since the death of his friends. For the first time in his life, he looked his age. She didn't want him worrying about her.

"I'm not worried about Blake. I'm just not sure how well suited I am to being a wife," Angel admitted.

"What do you mean?"

"I've always been independent and gone my own way. My art has been my life. I know nothing about running a household, of being a wife, of making someone happy."

"Just be yourself, Angel. That's all anyone can do."

"It would be different if Blake loved me, Harry. He would be more tolerant of me."

"And what makes you think he doesn't love you?"

She glanced at him, startled by his question. "Of course he doesn't love me. You know better than anyone why Blake is marrying me."

Harry nodded. "Yes, I know why Blake *thinks* he's marrying you. I don't think he has any idea how he feels about you. You see, Blake was never encouraged to show his emotions as a young child. He learned early in life to bury them. Even after Lydia died, he continued to distrust his emotions and ignore them, just as he is doing now.'' Harry gave Angel a slight smile. "He's fascinated by you, Angel. He's never known anyone remotely like you. When he talks about you—which is quite often, by the way—he's wistful. It's as though he's drawn to your beauty and vivaciousness but doesn't understand it. Try to understand him, Angel. He needs lots of it. Perhaps eventually he will be able to understand himself.''

They pulled up in front of the church. Blake was standing near the front steps talking with Jeremy. When Blake saw the car he immediately broke off the conversation and strode to the curb.

"Hello," he said, opening the door and helping Angel out of the car. She had decided that, since this would be her one and only wedding, she would wear white. She certainly had the right to do so. Her dress was street length, lace over satin, and she wore a tiny hat that cupped around her head, leaving her hair to fall loosely to her shoulders.

Blake looked marvelous in his formal clothes. She glanced down at what he held in his hand, then looked up inquiringly.

He glanced down at his hand, and his color darkened slightly. "I wanted to be sure you had flowers," he said, handing her a small arrangement of white rosebuds, pink sweetheart roses and baby's breath.

Angel buried her nose in them, trying to find something to say. She was touched by his thoughtfulness and bemused by the information Harry had given her in the car.

Blake led her over to where Jeremy waited.

"You are truly a beautiful Angel today," Jeremy commented gallantly. "Blake is a very lucky man."

Angel could feel her color deepening. She wondered if Blake had admitted to Jeremy the reason behind the marriage. She glanced up at Blake from beneath her lashes.

He had turned away and was speaking to Harry. Whatever he thought, it was well hidden. Once again he was the aloof, quiet businessman she had first met.

"Thank you, Jeremy."

Blake glanced around and saw the warm expressions on the faces of his best friend and his intended bride and felt a pain somewhere in the region of his chest. He felt left out somehow, and he walked over and put his arm around her.

"The pastor is waiting for us, if you're ready."

Angel smiled. "Yes."

When Angel looked up at him with that warm expression in her beautiful eyes Blake recognized that he would willingly do anything for her. The thought panicked him. Angel was marrying him so that he could keep control of the business. Theirs was not a love match. He was being an idiot to think differently. The pretense in front of his friends had almost become real. Was he losing his mind and actually falling for her?

Of course not. He was attracted to her, but he wasn't in love with her. Blake forced his emotions back to their proper place in his scheme of things—they no longer mattered.

Blake and Angel were married in the small chapel with Harry and Jeremy their only witnesses. Blake provided matching wedding bands and Angel fought the tears that came to her eyes when she thought of her father, who had wanted to make sure she married and was taken care of. *Oh, Papa, if only you were here with me now. Tell me what to do. Tell me how to be a wife to Blake. I want this marriage to work.*

After the vows were exchanged, they were pronounced man and wife and Blake was told to kiss the bride. She looked up at him and Blake felt as though a hand had squeezed his heart.

A shaft of sunlight shone through a stained-glass window, showering her with myriad colors, bathing her in an iridescent glow. She gazed up at him with shyness and he slowly pulled her into his arms. She felt so good there. Tilting her chin with his finger, he placed his lips on hers and sealed the union with a silent vow to treat her gently and with kindness so that she would never be sorry for the sacrifice she was making—marrying a man she didn't love.

Angel's heart was thumping so strongly it shook her whole body with every beat. She was now Mrs. Blake Carlyle—for better or for worse, for richer or for poorer. And when he kissed her, she thought her knees were going to buckle. His touch was even more potent than she had remembered and she had not forgotten a single instant they had spent together.

Her mouth softened and opened to his as though made for him and Blake felt the response in his own body.

His arms slackened and he turned back to the pastor and offered his hand. "Thank you for your time, sir."

The man smiled. "I'm glad to be of service. Performing marriages is one of the more positive parts of my duties. I always enjoy them." He took Angel's hand. "Mrs. Carlyle, I wish you the very best and my blessings go with you both."

Harry cleared his throat. "Well, if that's all that needs to be done, I have to get back to the office."

His prosaic comment reduced the tension in the air and they all laughed.

"I certainly wouldn't want to keep you from important business, Harry," Angel teased.

"I didn't mean it that way. I'm just sorry you wouldn't let me hold a reception for you."

Jeremy spoke up. "Well, I'm going to allow the newlyweds their honeymoon, and when they return, we are going to have one hell of a party."

"But Jeremy—" Blake started to say.

"I don't want to hear it." Jeremy held up his hand. "The deed is done, arrangements have been made. The only thing you two need to do is show up." He clapped Blake on the back, almost knocking him off balance. "Don't let us keep you. I'm sure you have all kinds of plans for the rest of the day." He laughed, the innuendo obvious, and Blake knew that was the reason he hadn't wanted a reception today. He hadn't wanted to stand around and listen to all the sage advice of his friends. Not with Angel. Maybe later the comments wouldn't be so obvious. He could only hope. The reasons for the marriage were beginning to come back to haunt him.

After they waved the two men goodbye, Blake and Angel got into Blake's car. He turned towards her, his arm resting on the back of the seat. "Are you hungry?"

She shook her head.

"Neither am I. I never realized how nerve-racking getting married could be."

His wry comment caused Angel to relax somewhat. He seemed so calm that she had assumed he was already planning his next day at the office.

"I thought we might drive down the coast this week, if you would like. Have you seen much of it?"

"Not since I was very young. Papa used to take me on various trips the summers I visited."

"There's a very nice resort about four hours south of here, located on the coast. I thought we could stay there tonight."

"I'd like that."

He picked up a lock of hair that was curling

around her shoulder. It felt like silk and he curled it around his hand. "Do you have a bag packed?"

She nodded.

"Why don't we go pick it up and give you a chance to change clothes?"

"How about you?"

He glanced down at his suit and shrugged. "I'm fine."

"Thank you for the beautiful church service, Blake. I thought everything turned out very well."

His gaze returned to her. "Thank you for marrying me. You make a beautiful bride. Jeremy was right. You look like an angel."

Angel flushed at his words. She had just received her very first compliment from Blake. He seemed to be just as uncomfortable as she was. "Thank you, Blake." She glanced around. "Shouldn't we be going?"

Blake straightened and started the car. "Good idea. I wanted to get to the resort before dark, if possible."

During the scenic drive south Angel began to think about the night ahead of them. Would Blake make love to her? She wasn't sure how she felt about the subject. He was her husband, and the purpose of the marriage was to have a child. There was no reason to postpone intimacy, but she couldn't tell from his expression what Blake was thinking and she didn't have the courage to ask.

Suzanne and Michelle had given her an outrageously expensive nightgown for her wedding night. She had tried it on and blushed. It was gossamer thin. Except for a tie on either side of the waist, the gown was open from shoulder to ankle on each side. Angel wondered if she dare wear it that night. Forcing herself to concentrate on the breathtaking scenery, Angel refused to anticipate the events of the next few hours.

Dinner was over and Blake and Angel sat in front of a large bay window, enjoying the view of the Pacific Ocean as it rolled relentlessly toward the shore, breaking on the boulders scattered along the way, then ebbing back to sea.

Neither had had much of an appetite and Angel sipped on her after-dinner liqueur, hoping it would relax her.

"Are you tired?" Blake finally broke their shared silence.

"A little."

"Are you ready to go upstairs?"

She caught her lower lip between her teeth for a moment, then nodded. She wished she had all the experience he attributed to her. He was going to discover soon enough that she had less experience than most high-school girls. Would he be bored with her?

Blake took her hand, surprised to feel how cold it

was. He gripped it firmly and escorted her through the lobby and to the elevator.

Once in their room, Blake went over to the fireplace and began to build a small fire. Angel tried to ignore the massive king-size bed and concentrated on watching him.

He glanced around. "Go ahead and make use of the bathroom, if you'd like."

Angel gathered up her gown and robe, disappeared behind the bathroom door. Perhaps a soaking bath would help to relax her.

It did. The combination of the warm water and the alcoholic beverages she had consumed during and after her meal almost put her to sleep, and she slipped into her gown and robe with lazy, somnolent movements. When she opened the bathroom door Angel found Blake sitting in his shirt sleeves and slacks in front of the fire. He glanced up and smiled.

"Feel better?" She looked like a child standing there, her hair in a tousled topknot.

"Yes. I can barely keep my eyes open."

He stood up. "Come sit here by the fire while I shower." He took her hand and led her to the small love seat he had been occupying. He leaned over and kissed her cheek. "I'll be right back."

Angel soon became mesmerized by the flickering firelight, her mind drifting lazily, random thoughts coming and going.

She heard the bathroom door open and casually

glanced around. Angel caught her breath. Blake walked out, still towel-drying his hair, wearing nothing but a small pair of briefs that emphasized more than they concealed. His body was bronzed, with hard, well-toned muscles rippling with the movement of his hands and arms. Dressed, Blake was impressive. Stripped, he took her breath away. He nonchalantly sat down beside her.

"Enjoying the fire?"

"Very much."

He grinned with wry amusement. "I'm glad. I was afraid you might fall asleep."

"I don't think there was ever a danger of that."

He stood up, pulling her to her feet. "Do you really need this robe?" he asked, gently untying the sash.

Mute, she shook her head.

He slid his hands to her shoulders and pushed the smooth material off her arms so that it fell in a satin circle around her feet. His breath caught in his throat. Bathed in the soft reflection of firelight, Angel looked like part of the flames with her bright hair and fair skin. Her gown was so sheer that it scarcely made a shadow anywhere on her. He tried not to think about the number of men who had seen her like that.

Without a word Blake picked her up in his arms and carried her over to the bed. The covers were folded back and he lowered her onto the pillow.

Reaching for the ribbon that held her hair, he untied it, then spread the rich tones of flame through his fingers and down around her shoulders.

Her eyes seemed unusually large in her face and if he didn't know better Blake would have said her expression was apprehensive. Stretching out beside Angel, he gently turned her toward him. Her gown fell open, exposing the warm curve of her hip and thigh. He leaned up on his elbow, taking in the picture she made of innocent seductiveness. His hand began to stroke along her hip, back and forth between her waist and thigh. He skin felt like satin and he could feel the slight ripple of nerves wherever he touched her.

Slowly he leaned toward her, kissing her on her nose, cheek and lips. He could feel her starting to relax and he took his time, wanting her to enjoy their time together.

The gown got in the way of his explorations and he sat up, tugging it gently from her. He stopped her when she reached for the sheet. "I want to see you, Angel," he explained in a husky voice. The glow from the fireplace lovingly emphasized the curves and hollows of the woman beside him.

Slowly he began kissing her, the light, affectionate caresses eventually deepening into long, soul-searching expressions of possession.

Angel was soon lost in the sensations Blake was creating. She could feel her bones and muscles sink limply into the waiting bed. His hands seemed to know just how to evoke a response from her and she shivered with the unfamiliar feelings.

"Are you cold?" he whispered, his lips sliding across her cheek to her ear.

"No. I feel as though I'm burning up."

She could feel more than hear his chuckle. "I don't want you to catch a cold due to overexposure." He placed his thigh over her, his knee resting comfortably between her legs.

Angel felt his arousal against her. She didn't have to wonder if he wanted her. If only she knew how to let him know she wanted him, too. Her hands hesitantly stroked across his chest and down his abdomen. She felt him quiver at her touch. He reached down and removed his last article of clothing, giving her silent permission to caress him.

He groaned when her hand brushed against him and she jerked away, uncertain. Then he shifted so that he was kneeling between her legs.

Blake had waited for months for this moment and could wait no longer. He wanted Angel so badly he shook with it. Lowering himself against her, Blake's mouth found hers once again, his tongue imitating the movements of lovemaking, his arms holding her tightly against him.

Angel's arms crept up around his neck and she gave herself up to him, knowing that Blake Carlyle was the man she had been waiting for all her life, at peace because she had waited for him to show her the intricate mysteries of lovemaking.

Blake suddenly pulled his head back and stared down at her in confusion. She smiled up at him with trusting innocence.

"Angel?" He was bewildered. All of his preconceived ideas had just gone up in smoke. Blake had discovered that his new bride was a virgin.

Chapter Seven

A fierce surge of protective possession flooded Blake as he acknowledged the implications of his discovery. All of his imaginings of Angel with other men had been wrong. Her look of innocence had not been faked. She had never given herself to another man.

Until now. She had given herself to him. She had responded to his lovemaking, allowing him intimacies that no other man had known.

Blake was inundated with such intense emotion he felt as though he were drowning in sensation.

Angel felt him pause and forced herself to relax. Suzanne had told her the first time might be uncomfortable unless she relaxed.

Her arms tightened. Blake deepened their kiss at

the same time he took possession of her. After a brief moment of discomfort Angel was aware of nothing else but Blake. Tiny pinpricks of light seemed to burst within her, causing her to respond to his rhythm with a slight arching of her back. She felt so protected, wrapped securely in his arms. He paused, his mouth blazing a burning trail down her neck to her breast, and Angel forgot to breathe. The tiny lights began to grow larger within her until they suddenly burst into flames, wrapping them both in incandescent light.

"Oh, Blake," she murmured when she could catch her breath.

Once again his mouth found hers and he held her to him until he brought them both to a peak where they tumbled into a sea of sensuous satisfaction.

Angel had found her home—in Blake's arms.

She turned over several hours later, feeling chilled. Reaching for Blake she found nothing but an empty pillow. Angel sat up, bewildered. Faint moonlight cast shadows in the room and she saw Blake standing at the window, staring out. The fire had gone out and the room was cool.

"Aren't you cold?" she asked softly.

He glanced around in surprise. He returned to the bed and sat down beside her. Reaching out he rubbed her cheek with his forefinger. "Not really. Are you?"

She nodded and he grinned. He crawled back under the covers. "Would you like me to get you warm again?" he asked in a teasing voice.

"Why were you awake?"

"Couldn't sleep," he whispered, pulling her close and stroking her with long, slow movements, down her back, along her side, smoothing her hair from her face.

"Why not?"

"It doesn't matter." His mouth found hers and she was soon lost in the pleasure of Blake's lovemaking once more.

Once Angel was asleep again, curled up trustingly on his shoulder, Blake lay there, holding her close to his side, thinking.

He had made love to many women in his lifetime, but he had never experienced what he had felt that night. It scared the hell out of him. What was it about Angel that affected him so?

They had known each other since she was born, yet they didn't know each other at all. All his preconceived ideas about her had to be readjusted. He had accepted her willingness to marry him and have his child without question. Until now.

Blake wanted to understand her. For the first time in his life he wanted to get close to another person. And he didn't know how. And what if, once he got close to her, she hurt him? Could he live with that?

He wasn't at all sure. He didn't want to need her

in his life if she were going to leave him after a year or two. He needed to remember that he had offered that option to her. He had honestly thought he could make a logical, objective decision to fulfill the stipulation without becoming emotionally involved. He was a fool.

Blake was ready to acknowledge that he was definitely emotionally involved with Angel.

When Angel woke up the next morning she could hear the shower running. She smiled and stretched, wincing a little at the unexpected soreness. Blake had been wonderful to her the night before—tender and caring, gentle and so very loving. She found that very reassuring.

She heard the water stop and waited expectantly for him to appear. She didn't have long to wait. He came into the room clad only in a well-worn pair of jeans. Barefooted and bare chested, with his hair tousled, Blake looked marvelous to Angel.

"Good morning," they said in unison, then laughed.

"Are you ready for breakfast?" he asked, his gaze taking in the slight flush on her cheeks.

"Give me fifteen minutes and I will be." She glanced around the room. "Would you hand me my robe, please?"

He found her modesty endearing and refused to tease her about it. As a matter of fact, he found everything about Angel enchanting. He gave her the robe and leaned down and kissed her soundly. "Are you ready to start your sight-seeing of the coast, Mrs. Carlyle?"

Never had Angel seen him so lighthearted. The lines were gone from his forehead and around his eyes. He looked happy and rested. She returned his smile.

"Anytime you are, Mr. Carlyle."

"We'll leave right after breakfast."

The trip down the coastline of southern California seemed to have a magical quality about it. Had the weather ever been so perfect? Everyone they met was kind, everywhere they went they found happiness. Or was it possible that they provided their own?

They took long walks on several beaches, spent hours wandering through the seaside resorts, finding souvenirs and enjoying the sun. With Angel's delicate coloring she had to use a heavy sunscreen in order not to burn, and Blake professed an acute interest in making sure she was carefully covered with the sunscreening lotion.

One day they visited Solvang, an authentic-looking Danish village, complete with windmills, in the Santa Ynez Valley north of Santa Barbara. Angel was entranced with the small shops and the calorie-laden pastries. Blake appeared content to wander along beside her, holding her hand and enjoying her ever-changing expressions.

While eating at one of the sidewalk cafés Angel nodded to a family walking past. "Did you notice the little girl in Danish costume?"

"She's very pleased with herself, isn't she?"

"Oh, yes!" Angel laughed delightedly. "Wasn't she a doll? I bet she isn't much past two. What do you think?"

"I have no idea," Blake admitted.

"Neither do I."

Blake leaned forward, his forearm brushing against hers. "Well, if you hadn't given your litter away, you would have had plenty of practical knowledge by now." His eyes danced with mischief.

Angel had the grace to blush and she refused to meet his gaze.

Blake began to laugh. "A litter. I couldn't believe what I was hearing!"

"Well," Angel explained with a trace of defensiveness, "you made me angry."

"I realize that. I might have believed you if you hadn't used the word 'litter.'" He shook his head, chuckling.

Angel watched him with a slight pang somewhere in the region of her heart. Relaxed and smiling as he was, Blake looked devastating. She wondered how long she had been in love with him. It had happened imperceptibly over the past few months. What would life be like if Blake were to fall in love with her and their marriage became more than a fulfillment of their fathers' wishes?

She could only hope that someday she might find out.

Another day Angel spent painting while Blake relaxed, watched and later napped. The serene countryside had caught her imagination, and the spirited horses in a nearby pasture enticed her to pause and attempt to capture them on canvas.

When they checked into a large hotel overlooking the ocean that night, Blake brought up her art. "You're really very good, aren't you? Your painting has such a vibrancy to it. I had no idea you were so talented."

Angel had been brushing her hair and she stopped and turned away from the mirror. Blake sat on a sofa in front of the large window overlooking the view of the ocean. He had turned and was leaning his chin on his forearm, which rested on the back of the sofa.

"You really mean that, don't you?"

"Yes, I really do. I'm ashamed to admit that I was surprised. Your ability to catch the playfulness and freedom of the horses and their colts today amazed me. Have you sold any of your work?"

"Some," she admitted cautiously.

"I'm sure it will sell very well in this area."

"I'm hoping so, too," she said slowly, walking over to him. She wondered if she should tell him about her show planned for the following month.

Perhaps it would be better to explain to him once it was set up. He had probably never even heard of AB, but seeing her paintings in a local gallery might be a nice surprise for him.

She decided to wait to tell him.

Angel leaned over the sofa and kissed him. Before she knew what was happening he had pulled her over the back of the seat and onto his lap, where he proceeded to kiss her thoroughly. Angel found this side of his nature so surprising. He appeared so cool and self-contained but during the past week he had been warm and passionate and wonderful. He looked rested and content and seemed to have gotten in the habit of smiling. Dimples that she was sure few people knew existed had appeared in his cheeks. He had developed a hearty appetite, including the one he was trying to appease at the moment.

Angel pushed back from him a few inches. "I thought we were going to go eat."

"We are." He began nibbling on her ear.

"I mean now."

"Now? You'd leave me in this condition for the next hour or more?"

"But you're always in that condition."

He laughed at her injured tone. "It certainly seems that way when I'm around you." He eased her off his lap. "All right. Never let it be said that I am not the complete gentleman. If you are hungry, then of course I'll feed you."

She glanced up at him, tilting her head slightly. "Then again, they'll still be serving dinner for several hours yet. I don't suppose I'm *that* hungry."

Blake reached for her again, kissing her on the ear, then the neck, and finally searching for and possessing her mouth.

They were the last couple served for dinner that night.

It was late Sunday evening when Blake and Angel arrived back in San Francisco. Their week together seemed more like a dream to Angel. She hated to see it end.

When they walked in the front door of Blake's family home Angel stopped in the foyer and looked around in amazement. She hadn't been in the house for years but she remembered it as very dark and somber. Now it was full of light and color.

"Blake, this is beautiful. How long has it been this way?"

"They just finished with it. I thought you would prefer it."

"You mean you had this redone for me?"

"Mmm-hmm." He took her hand and started toward the stairs. "Might as well show you everything." He went down a long hallway lined with doors, stopped in front of one and opened it to reveal another flight of steps. At the top another door stood open, inviting them in. He entered the room first, flipped on the light and turned around, watching her face.

Blake had rebuilt the top floor, tearing out the smaller partitions and creating a loft effect with a giant skylight.

"Oh, Blake," she said softly, the lump in her throat making it almost impossible for her to talk. He had remodeled his home for her, even though he had never taken her painting all that seriously. "I could have used my studio, you know."

"I thought you'd find this more convenient."

She threw her arms around his neck. "Oh, I do. Thank you so much." Angel stood on her toes and kissed him fiercely.

He smiled. "Actually, I had an ulterior motive. I never did like the idea of you and Jean-Pierre working in such close harmony."

Angel laughed. "Don't be silly. You almost sound jealous."

"I do, don't I?" Blake agreed with a grin. "What do you know." He picked her up and started down the stairway. "Your other surprise can wait until morning."

"What is it?"

"If I tell you, it won't be a surprise."

"So who cares? What is it?"

"I thought you should have your own transportation, so I got you a small car to run around in."

"What kind of a small car? A Renault? A Volkswagen?"

"A Mercedes coupe."

"Blake!"

"I told the dealer I wanted it in sapphire blue. I didn't think I could match the color of your hair, so settled for your eyes."

"That has to be the most romantic thing anyone has ever done for me."

"That's not romantic. You needed transportation. I was just being practical."

"Of course you were."

"Aren't you ready to go to bed yet?" he asked hopefully.

She tightened her arms around his neck as he pushed the door open to his bedroom. "Oh, yes. I am absolutely exhausted," she said with a tiny smile playing around her lips.

"Oh." He tried to hide his disappointment.

She started laughing. "Not *that* exhausted, Blake," she added, and they ended up on the bed together in a flurry of clothes and bed covers. Blake gave Angel a very warm and encouraging welcome home.

Angel was in her studio the next day when Foster, who had run the household for years, tapped on the door.

"You have a phone call, Mrs. Carlyle. Miss Marcia Sinclair."

Angel glanced around in surprise. "She asked to speak to *me*?"

Foster's expression remained impassive. "That is correct."

Hastily cleaning her hands, she picked up the phone. "H'lo?"

"Angel. I hope I'm not interrupting you," Marcia said in a hesitant voice.

"That's all right."

"I was calling to see if you and Blake were going to be home this evening."

"As far as I know."

A slight note of excitement crept into Marcia's voice. "I would very much like to bring your wedding gift over. I can't wait to show you what I found!"

How could anyone dislike Marcia? Angel had easily spotted what Blake enjoyed about her. She was a genuinely sincere person. Angel would have found her position more comfortable if she could have disliked the woman, but unfortunately for her peace of mind, that wasn't the case.

"Certainly, Marcia. Could you make it around eight o'clock? Blake should be home by then."

"Fine. I'll see you both then."

"What do you mean, Marcia will be here in a few minutes?" Blake stared at Angel as though she had just announced the bombing and total destruction of the Golden Gate bridge.

"I'm afraid your caveman tactics when you first got home tonight completely distracted me. I forgot all about her phone call."

They had finished their meal and were sitting in the library drinking coffee. Angel had been reassured by Blake's homecoming that evening. He had scooped her up in his arms and carried her to their bedroom, muttering about how much he had missed her all day, almost as though he was irritated with the idea. She had missed him, too, and had responded to him with loving fervor.

Blake frowned. "I don't understand why you invited her over here."

"She said she had a wedding gift for us and wanted to bring it right away. I could see no reason to be rude to her."

Blake got up and went over to the bar. Angel thought she heard him mutter, "Just what I need," but she wasn't sure.

She walked over to him. "Does it bother you to see her?"

Bother him? No. But Marcia was a reminder of a situation he hadn't handled well. He felt embarrassed, inadequate and uncomfortable.

The doorbell rang and Angel went to the door.

Blake hadn't answered her but from the expression on his face the thought of Marcia was painful to him.

Angel opened the door with a smile, then almost winced. Marcia looked stunning in a brilliant red dress that enhanced her dark hair and complexion. Her eyes shone and her cheeks were slightly flushed.

"Come in, Marcia." She motioned her toward the library. "I was just telling Blake that you planned to stop by."

Marcia carried a large, flat, wrapped package and she carefully lowered it to the floor, leaning it against a chair, then slowly turned around and faced Blake.

"Hello, Blake," she said with a hesitant smile.

Blake nodded. "It's good to see you again, Marcia. You're looking well. How's Richard?"

She shrugged slightly. "Father is always the same. You know how he is."

"Yes."

The look on Marcia's face caused Angel to stop breathing for a moment. Despite the routine conversation, Marcia's face glowed with love. Blake would have to be blind not to see it—and he was a very discerning man.

"I still can't believe my luck," Marcia began. She motioned to the package on the floor. "I found it tucked away in a small shop. The owner had no idea what he had. Otherwise I probably couldn't have afforded it." She stopped and clasped her hands in back of her as though unsure of herself. "I hope you like it."

Angel glanced at Blake, wishing she knew what he was thinking. He had the darnedest ability to mask his thoughts. At the moment he appeared more like the stranger she married than the man she had spent the previous week with.

She tore the paper away and began to unwrap what was obviously a large painting.

"I thought you might want it for your den, Blake. It would look perfect over the fireplace," Marcia suggested. "I hoped it would be a nice finishing touch to all the remodeling you've been doing."

When Angel uncovered the painting she froze.

Marcia nervously continued her monologue. "Yes, it is actually an AB original. Isn't it marvelous? I understand it's one of his earlier works but you can see the genius there, can't you?" She smiled at Angel. "Knowing how much you are interested in art, I wanted to give you both something you could enjoy."

Angel didn't know what to do. What did you say to someone who gave you one of your own paintings for a wedding present?

Marcia walked over to Blake, touching his arm slightly. "I've saved the best news for last. The artist AB is having a showing of his paintings here in San Francisco next month and I managed to get tickets for the preopening showing." She reached into her purse and pulled out two tickets. "I thought it was the least I could do to welcome Angel to San Francisco."

Angel knew she had to get out of there for a few minutes. She needed to think. Quickly gathering up the wrappings she glanced at Marcia, then at Blake. "I don't know what to say," she said in complete honesty. "I'm overwhelmed." Going to the door she muttered, "I'll be right back," hoping the paper in her arms gave her a good enough reason to leave them.

As soon as the door closed behind her, Marcia turned to Blake. "Are you upset with me for coming over?"

He shook his head. "Not at all. I appreciate your thoughtfulness. The picture is very beautiful."

"Oh, Blake, please don't pretend with me. I can't stand the polite aloofness." She walked over to him. "You don't have to keep up the pretense with me any longer. You see, I know."

"You know what?"

"Why you married Angel."

"I don't know what you're talking about."

"Oh, Blake, you know how Father is. He wouldn't leave it alone. He couldn't understand why you suddenly decided to marry, particularly so soon after the death of your father."

Blake stiffened. She took his hand and squeezed it. "Father found out about the agreement your father made with Angel's. I know why you married her and I want you to know that I understand."

I wish to hell I did, he thought with painful introspection. *I wish I could understand why I can't keep my mind off her.*

"I'll wait for you, Blake, however long it takes. I would wait forever if I thought I could be with you again."

He stared at Marcia with alarm. "But, Marcia, you don't understand—"

"Yes, I do. I understand you don't love her and that she probably doesn't love you. I've thought about all of the circumstances so much. I can't see her staying here in San Francisco permanently, can you?"

Marcia had touched on the haunting fear that seemed to accompany Blake lately.

"I don't know," he admitted finally.

"Just remember that I'll be here."

Angel heard Marcia's last remark when she reentered the room and saw the look of pain on Blake's face. What had she interrupted? She was very much afraid she didn't want to know.

"I asked Foster for some fresh coffee. It should be in shortly." Angel had decided to tell them who she was. There was no reason to keep the secret any longer. Mr. Huntington had pleaded with her to consider announcing her identity at the show and she had decided to do so. It was only fair that she tell

Marcia, since she'd given them the painting and the tickets.

Except Marcia didn't give her the chance.

"Oh, I'm sorry, but I can't stay," she said nervously. "I have to get back home and help my father entertain some business acquaintances from out of town." She glanced at Blake, then at Angel. "I just wanted you to have the painting."

"Thank you," Blake said gently, wishing there was some way to let her know that even if Angel left him, he knew that he and Marcia could never take up where their relationship had left off.

Angel heard the gentleness in his voice and wanted to cry. What an abominable situation they were in. It was obvious that both she and Marcia loved Blake, and she was beginning to think that whatever emotions he had were being pulled between the two of them.

Blake walked Marcia to the door and leaned over and kissed her gently on the cheek. "Don't wait for me, Marcia. I'm not worth the sacrifice. You're going to make a very deserving man a marvelous wife."

She smiled up at him, her eyes filled with tears. "Good night, Blake."

He watched her get into her car, the continuing sense of inadequacy nagging at him. He cared about her, but he didn't love her. And the woman that he wanted to love him more than anything in the world had married him only to fulfill an agreement.

Angel was waiting for him when he returned to the library. In a deliberately bright voice, she said, "I can see that my secret is no longer safe and I might as well confess."

"What are you talking about?"

"I am the painter known as AB. I've used my initials and the sign of a halo to identify my paintings. I had no idea what to say to Marcia just now. Should I have told her who I am, do you think?"

Blake stared at her in shock, then walked over to the painting and studied it. "Unbelievable."

"But true."

"Then you are having a showing here in San Francisco?"

"Yes. I spent the entire time I was in Paris painting like a fiend trying to prepare for it. I've got to meet with the proprietor of the gallery sometime this week to make final arrangements."

"He's tall, very distinguished looking?"

"You saw us at the restaurant, didn't you?"

"Yes."

"Why didn't you say something?"

"I didn't believe it was any of my business," he said coolly, and Angel stared at him in disbelief.

His tone had reminded her of the man she had first known, and it hurt. No matter how warm and affectionate he was to her, she needed to remember that Blake Carlyle would never allow his emotions to get in the way of his behavior.

She shivered at the thought. He was still the ruthless businessman. She should never forget that. And she should continue to remember why they had married.

A chill had come into the room and Angel had no intention of teasing Blake into warming her up, a joke that they had kept going during the past week.

Her emotions were totally involved with him, but she recognized that he would never allow himself to get that close to her. She almost felt sorry for Marcia. The woman was obviously in love with him. Angel wondered if Blake would be as cool and distant to her someday as he had been with Marcia.

As soon as she produced his child, he would no doubt feel their bargain was complete.

Chapter Eight

Within a few short weeks after their return to San Francisco, Blake and Angel seemed to be absorbed into their former lives, their marriage scarcely causing a ripple in their usual routine. Blake continued to work long hours and came home distracted and quiet. Angel hesitated to take up his time with stories regarding the busy schedule she was maintaining in order to prepare for her art show.

The truth was that neither one knew how to behave toward the other.

Blake was uncomfortable with all the unfamiliar emotions Angel stirred up in him. He didn't know how to deal with them. Therefore, he reverted to past behavior—he pushed them out of his mind and forced himself to concentrate on the company. Unfortunately his ability to concentrate seemed to have dwindled during the past few weeks.

In the middle of a conference he would suddenly picture Angel lying in bed, waiting for him, or hear her laughter or remember her teasing smile and he would have to force his attention back to the business at hand. She seemed to have turned his brain to gelatin.

Angel seldom told him how she spent her days. He assumed she was busy with her show but he was afraid if he asked too many questions she would feel he was checking up on her. He had promised her she would retain her independence, that their marriage would not change her life-style. He didn't want her to feel she had to answer to him. At the time that he agreed to her rules Blake had had no idea how difficult it would be for him to live up to them.

Meanwhile, Angel decided after a few weeks that Blake was bored with her. They shared only the most casual conversation. It was only at night when he hungrily reached for her that Angel felt Blake might not be sorry they had married. Even then she sometimes wondered if he was hoping to make sure she became pregnant as soon as possible. She had a hunch that once Blake decided on a plan of action, he became wholeheartedly involved.

She didn't know what she would have done if Jean-Pierre had not been there. He helped her by running errands, hunting down frame shops, encouraging her, insisting she eat when she forgot about meals. He accompanied her to the galleries and to meetings with Huntington, the owner of the gallery setting up her show. Slowly but surely everything was shaping up.

Jeremy was the first person to say something to Blake.

"What's happening on the home front these days? You haven't mentioned Angel in days." They were having lunch together and Blake pushed back his plate slightly at Jeremy's candid question.

"There's nothing much to mention. We're both busy. We don't see all that much of each other—not with the hours I keep."

"You're a fool."

"What are you talking about?"

"You are treating your marriage like some business merger. If I didn't know you so damned well I'd be tempted to believe the rumors circulating."

"What rumors?"

"That the only reason you married Angel was to get your hands on her stock."

Blake studied his friend impassively. "A rumor like that isn't too surprising under the circumstances. It's more or less to be expected. Everyone knows we didn't know each other long before we married."

"And neither of you are doing a damned thing to dispel the rumors. You spend every waking moment buried at your office and Angel's busy being seen all over town with an adoring Frenchman."

Blake stiffened. "What are you talking about?"

"Don't tell me you don't know! They're seen everywhere together—going in and out of art galleries and museums, lunching, strolling along Fisherman's Wharf carrying on animated conversations—in French, of course. Three people this past week have mentioned to me that they've seen them together. She's certainly doing nothing to hide the fact she's seeing someone else."

"Jean-Pierre."

"You mean you're aware of him?"

"He's a friend of hers visiting from France."

"And you don't even care? You really are a cold-blooded bastard, aren't you, Blake? Maybe the rumors are true. So long as you have the stock, you don't care what she's doing." Jeremy threw down his napkin in disgust. "You know, I've always thought that cool, aloof image of yours was a facade. I was wrong. You have a calculator for a heart and a computer for a brain. You don't need people—either friends or a wife." He pushed back his chair. "Sorry to have taken up so much of your valuable time."

Blake stood up with Jeremy. "Hey, fella, hold on. I may not have the emotional responses you're looking for, but you're exploding like a Fourth-of-July fireworks display that was accidentally touched off all at once. Calm down a minute and let's talk, okay?"

Jeremy stared at his friend for a moment, then with a sheepish expression slowly sat down. Blake signaled for more coffee and waited for the beverage to be poured before he spoke.

"I didn't mean to give you the impression that I don't care what Angel is doing. I do. Very much. It's just that our agreement when we married was that I wouldn't put any restrictions on her. Angel needs her freedom. She knows she can return to France if she isn't happy here. I want her to be happy and stay. So I don't want to play the heavy-handed husband and start making demands she won't tolerate."

"Even to allowing her to continue her relationship with her lover?"

"Jean-Pierre isn't her lover."

"How the hell can you possibly know that?"

"Because I know Angel and she would not break her word. She is very loyal."

"I can't believe this conversation."

"Just because I can calmly discuss Angel and her relationship with Jean-Pierre doesn't mean that I'm handling my feelings all that great," Blake admitted wryly. "I'm jealous as hell."

"He says as he calmly sips his coffee! I can't believe you, Blake. Are you afraid of admitting you're human, with all the frail emotions that entails? I knew you watched too much *Star Trek* as a kid. You must have convinced yourself you're another Spock!"

Blake laughed. "I'm afraid you're wrong. I sometimes feel I'm eaten up inside. Phyllis is convinced I'm losing my mind."

"What would ever cause your loyal secretary to see you as anything less than perfect?"

"When I dictated a letter that she brought back in to me and questioned. I told a client I would get back in touch with him as soon as I heard from Jean-Pierre. I meant to say Paul Schofield."

Jeremy grinned. "So you *have* been thinking of Angel and her friend."

"There's never a time when I'm not thinking about her, what she's doing, who see's seeing. I'm well aware that Jean-Pierre is still in the States. But she never mentions him, so I haven't brought him up, either."

"Have you told her how you feel?"

"Certainly not!"

"Too much pride?"

"No. Too much fear. I'm afraid to tell her what I'm feeling and what it's doing to me. If I end up issuing some crazy ultimatum, I'm not at all sure she would choose to stay with me."

"But that doesn't make any sense, Blake. If she loved you enough to marry you, why would she choose Jean-Pierre? She could have married him, you know."

"I've used that logic myself and would find it comforting but for one thing. Angel didn't marry me because she loved me."

"Then why the hell *did* she marry you?"

"I wish I knew. I have a hunch it was to please her father."

"How could marrying you please him when he's dead?"

"Our fathers made it clear they hoped we would marry."

"And good ol' levelheaded, serious-minded Blake wanted to fulfill their wishes. Don't give me that. I know you too well."

"I thought I knew myself, but my head's been whirling since Dad and Scott were killed."

"Looking at the situation objectively, I can certainly understand your willingness to sacrifice yourself on the altar of filial duty. Not many men would balk at claiming the luscious Angel as their own, all to appease their family's expectations. It was a tough job, but what the hell—what's that old saying, 'I could not love thee half so well, if not honor more'? Or something like that."

"I'm sure you find it all very amusing, but I happen to be in love with Angel."

"You think I don't know that? She had you walking into doors and falling down stairwells a week after she arrived. Of course you're in love with her, dolt! But you sure as hell don't act like it and I have a sneaky hunch you've never bothered to tell her, either."

"We don't have that sort of relationship."

"Oh, I can believe that. From the way you're behaving, you probably haven't gotten past the hand-holding stage yet."

Blake flushed slightly. "Oh, we've managed to progress further than that."

"Thank God. I, too, was beginning to doubt your sanity." He leaned closer, speaking in a confidential tone. "Will you take some advice from an old friend? Go home and tell your wife you love her and that you're jealous as hell that she's spending so much time with that French guy. You've got to tell her how you feel, man. It's the only way."

"Maybe you're right, Jeremy."

"I know I'm right. 'Faint heart never won fair lady.' You've already won her. You just forgot to claim her."

"I don't know what to do, Jean-Pierre," Angel finally admitted one afternoon while they walked along one of the paths in the beautifully laid-out Chinese gardens. "He shows no interest in what I've been doing each day. He rarely gets home until nine o'clock every night—sometimes even later. And when I ask him how things are going for him, he puts me off with some vague answer."

"Angel, don't you think you may be overreacting

to the situation a little? He must be very busy to be putting in such long hours. Perhaps he's just tired and doesn't want to talk about his day."

"If only I knew what he was thinking. He never gives me a clue as to his feelings. Sometimes I find myself wanting to scream and shout at him in order to get a reaction."

"But you knew the sort of man he was when you married him," Jean-Pierre pointed out with undeniable logic.

Angel nodded dispiritedly. "Yes, I did. But he seemed so different on our honeymoon."

Jean-Pierre laughed. "No man should be judged by his behavior during his honeymoon. That would hardly be fair!"

She reluctantly smiled in response. "I mean that he was more open and friendly—we seemed to have so much to talk about, so much to share with each other. He seemed relaxed and happy. Lately he seems so distracted that even when he's home his mind seems to be somewhere else."

"Why, hello, Angel! I thought that was you!"

Angel glanced around in surprise. Marcia stood at the intersection of two paths, looking composed and very much in tune with spring in her lovely pastel-colored skirt and sweater.

"Hello, Marcia. I didn't see you."

Marcia's smile widened. "Oh, that's all right. I almost hated to interrupt, you seemed so engrossed in your conversation." Her gaze fell on Jean-Pierre. For some reason Angel felt reluctant to introduce them and knew her attitude to be ridiculous.

"Marcia, I would like you to meet a friend of mine visiting here from France, Jean-Pierre Armand. Jean-Pierre, this is Marcia Sinclair. I've been showing Jean-Pierre San Francisco," she explained.

"I'm so pleased to meet you. I've heard so much about you."

Jean-Pierre gave her a quizzical look, then took her proffered hand in his. "How do you do? How is it you have heard about me?"

Marcia laughed. "Oh, all of Blake's friends have been talking about the two of you. They don't understand the situation."

Angel felt a tremor of alarm. Had she been indiscreet in being seen with Jean-Pierre so much? Blake had never said anything to her. He never asked about Jean-Pierre, so she didn't bring him into their conversations.

"What situation?" Angel asked faintly.

"Why, the reason behind your marriage. I know about the will," she whispered, as though conspiring. "You both did what you had to do, which is understandable. But neither you nor Blake are allowing the situation to ruin your lives." She glanced at Jean-Pierre. "Do you intend to stay here in the States until Angel can return to France with you?"

Jean-Pierre stared at the woman as though he had

lost his command of the English language and couldn't understand a word she said.

Angel understood only too well. Blake had told Marcia the truth about their marriage. No wonder he had told her she could return to France. He fully expected her to leave. He had never intended their marriage to be permanent. No wonder Marcia didn't seem to mind.

Her head seemed to be whirling with bits and pieces of conversations she had shared with Blake. She had heard only what she wanted to hear. She had interpreted his lovemaking to mean he wanted her to stay with him. How foolish of her! He had only been making sure she would be leaving as soon as possible!

Forcing herself to concentrate, she said, "I hope you will excuse us, Marcia. I have an appointment that I need to keep."

"Don't let me keep you." Marcia smiled at Jean-Pierre. "It was very nice to meet you. I hope to see you again sometime."

Angel watched her walk away as though a mist were forming around her.

"Angel, are you all right?" Jean-Pierre's voice seemed to come from far away. She would never be all right again.

By the time Jean-Pierre got her home Angel was shaking as though she had a hard chill. He suggested hot tea, and Foster agreed to bring it to the library.

"Sit down, little one, while I build a fire," Jean-Pierre said when they walked into the library.

"No! It's too warm for a fire."

"But you are so cold."

"I'll be all right. Just give me a few minutes."

"Why are you letting that silly woman upset you? Blake could not possibly prefer her to you."

"Oh, but he does. He always has. And to think I've felt sympathy for him for the long hours he keeps. No doubt he *must* be exhausted. He's probably been spending his evenings with her, then coming home to a wife he was obligated to get pregnant!"

"Angel! Stop it! You don't know what you're saying."

"I know exactly what I am saying. Blake never wanted to marry me. It was the only way he could hang on to the company. Our children will own the stock in the company. So he couldn't just marry me for my stock. He had to see that I produced a child for him. And the worst of it is that he told her about it after agreeing not to mention the real reason for our marriage to anyone. He told her that the only reason he was marrying me was for the stock in the company."

Jean-Pierre stared at her, stunned at the meaning of the words pouring like a torrent out of her mouth.

"But you love him."

"Oh, yes. I fell in love with him before I even returned to France. There were times during the first few weeks we were married that I hoped he was learning to love me, as well. But love was never part of the agreement. He doesn't want my love. He would be embarrassed if he thought I'd been so foolish as to fall in love with him." Tears flowed unchecked down her cheeks while she talked in a lifeless voice, all the vitality drained from her.

"Oh, Angel, my poor little one, it saddens me to see you in such pain."

She wrapped her arms around her waist, holding herself tightly, almost doubled over. The pain surged through her entire being like a tidal wave and she felt battered. Sobs began to shake her, and Jean-Pierre put his arms around her. "Hush, little one, you are only going to make yourself ill, carrying on this way."

But Angel no longer heard him. She was too wrapped up in the anguish of what she had learned about Blake and what she saw as her future. She also had to face the fact that her beloved father had created more grief in her life than she could stand.

Jean-Pierre poured a liberal amount of brandy in a glass and brought it to her. "Here, Angel, I want you to drink this," he said in a stern voice.

He held it to her mouth until she finished it, shuddering as the burning liquor found its way to her stomach.

"Why don't you lie down for a while?"

She shook her head, the tears continuing to flow.

Without waiting for permission, Jean-Pierre scooped her up into his arms and carried her into the foyer, just in time to meet Foster carrying a tea tray.

"Mrs. Carlyle is not feeling well. I'd like to put her to bed if I may. Perhaps you could direct me to her room."

Foster led the way upstairs to the bedroom Blake and Angel shared. He set the tray by the bed and turned down the covers.

Jean-Pierre gently laid her on the bed, then turned around to Foster.

"Do you know if she keeps any sedatives available?"

"I believe Mr. Blake was prescribed some tablets to help him sleep right after his father's death."

"Yes, that would work."

Foster disappeared into the adjoining bathroom, reappearing in a few minutes with a small bottle.

"Thank you."

Foster glanced at Angel lying on the bed, her face buried in the pillow. "Should we contact Mr. Blake, sir?"

Jean-Pierre smiled sardonically. "Under the present circumstances, Blake is probably the last person Angel wants to see."

Foster nodded his head and left the room, wondering what had happened to upset the young mistress but much too well bred to inquire.

Eventually Jean-Pierre coaxed Angel into drinking

some tea and swallowing one of the tablets. He sat and held her, patting her back and crooning softly. The strain of the past several months had finally caught up with her. Jean-Pierre was glad he didn't know how to contact Blake at the moment. His peaceable nature had been sorely tested. At the moment he could think of nothing more satisfying than the thought of beating Blake Carlyle to a bloody pulp.

Jean-Pierre sat with Angel until she fell asleep, holding her hand so that she knew he was there. He thought of the years he had known her, watched her mature and grow as a person, overcoming handicaps that a lesser woman would have allowed to stunt her emotionally or leave her embittered. Instead, Angel had made a crusade of being there for her friends, of loving them and tending to them, exhorting them to do their best.

Because of Angel's generosity in allowing him to stay at her home rent-free and introducing him to the contacts she had already made in the art world, Jean-Pierre would soon be able to return to France and marry Michelle, as they had planned for so many months. Angel had always been generous with everything but her heart—and, of course, her body. And now that she had given both to her husband he had shrugged them off as negligible.

Jean-Pierre shook his head sadly. He would do

anything in the world for Angel, but he knew of no way to patch her broken heart.

After his long luncheon with Jeremy, Blake was not in the mood to return to his office, but he made the effort and in a matter of hours delegated a considerable amount of work that had chained him to his desk in the past. He was, after all, only one person, and he had a life in addition to his corporate one. Blake wasn't sure why he had never faced that before, particularly since his father and Scott had made the subject their main topic of conversation on more than one occasion. Perhaps it had never seemed important to Blake before because there was nothing he would rather do than be engrossed in the intricacies of their thriving business.

Now that Angel had become part of his life, he no longer found the business consuming enough to forget her even briefly. He hoped that once he found a way to place their relationship on some sort of permanent basis he could relax and enjoy both sides of his life.

Glancing at his watch Blake decided to go home and talk with Angel—attempt to explain how he felt without offending her, ask her to spend more time with him, get her to share with him the details of her upcoming show. In short, let her know that he wanted very much to be included in every part of her life, if she would let him.

"I'll see you in the morning, Phyllis," he said, pausing by his secretary's desk.

She glanced up in surprise, then looked at the wall clock in shock. "Are you not feeling well, Blake?"

"I'm fine."

"I've never known you to go home by four o'clock before."

"I've decided to cut back on some of the hours I put in around here."

"Good for you. Have a good evening."

I certainly intend to, he thought to himself with a smile. Angel will probably think I've lost my mind, but she'll have to bear with me while I try to explain.

Foster was carrying a tea tray down the stairs when Blake let himself in the front door.

"Mr. Blake. You're home early. Are you not feeling well?"

"Do I have to be sick to come home at a decent hour, Foster?" he asked irritably. He supposed he had made rather a habit of his long hours.

"Why no, sir," Foster said formally. He glanced up the staircase uncertainly, then proceeded down the hallway to the kitchen with the tray.

Blake pulled off his tie and unbuttoned the top two buttons of his shirt. He wished he had asked Foster if Angel was home, but it didn't really matter. He would be here whenever she arrived. Pulling off his jacket he paused at the door of the library and looked in. She wasn't there. Maybe she was upstairs painting.

Taking the steps two at a time, his jacket held by one finger over his shoulder, Blake went upstairs. When he reached the top of the staircase he heard a door closing and turned the corner into the hallway expecting to see Angel.

Instead, he watched with stunned disbelief as Jean-Pierre turned away from the bedroom door and faced him. Blake had seen Jean-Pierre only once or twice since he arrived, and never had he seen him dressed so casually. He wore faded denim jeans and faded shirt with most of the buttons undone, showing a great deal of muscled chest. His shirt sleeves were rolled high on his arms, baring well-developed biceps, and Blake had a fleeting thought about the muscles necessary to do the kind of stone sculpture work Jean-Pierre preferred, before it really struck him what he was seeing. Jean-Pierre had been in the bedroom Blake shared with Angel.

Blake stared at the man, absently noting the mussed curls and the tired expression he wore. "What are you doing here?" Blake wasn't sure where the words came from. He was no longer thinking. Too many shocks were coming too closely together.

Jean-Pierre had calmed down from his initial reaction to Angel's despair. It was not his place to tell this man what a fool he was or what he thought of his despicable behavior. He now felt the less he said, the better.

"I've been taking care of your wife, since you obviously have other priorities," he said without pausing. He passed Blake and started down the stairs.

Blake whirled around. "Where's Angel?"

"In bed asleep. I would suggest you let her rest. She's had about all she can take today." Jean-Pierre had continued down the stairs while answering Blake without once looking back. In a few long strides, Jean-Pierre reached the front door and flung it open, slamming it behind him.

Never had Blake felt so much pain. Were the French so blasé about their affairs that they weren't even intimidated when the unsuspecting husband showed up early from work? Jean-Pierre hadn't even seemed embarrassed to be caught coming out of the bedroom.

I've been taking care of your wife, since you obviously have other priorities. My God! The man had his nerve. And what about Angel!

Blake retraced his steps and approached the closed bedroom door. Quietly he opened it. The drapes had been pulled and the room was shadowy. Silently he forced himself to move toward the bed. Angel was indeed asleep, her bright curls tousled and strewn across her pillow. Her face was in deeper shadow but she looked exhausted, and Blake withdrew, the pain deepening within him.

They must have spent the afternoon in bed together. What a fool he had been to think Angel was any different from her mother. Just because she was a virgin when he married her didn't mean she would not run to Jean-Pierre and pretend to be the poor neglected wife if the role suited her.

He wondered how hard it had been for her to pretend to enjoy his lovemaking and if she had spent the time comparing lovers.

Blake found himself in the library, having no clear idea how he had gotten there. His thoughts had shaken him. He had been systematically reviewing the ways of killing Jean-Pierre. Barehanded? But no, the man was too strong to succumb to him. A gun? A knife? Have him arrested? *For what, making love to my wife?*

I'm losing my mind, without a doubt, Blake decided with a deep groan. He sank into a chair and buried his head in his hands. What the hell did he do now? Confront her with the knowledge? Point out that he no longer wanted her for a wife, since she obviously shared the morals of an alley cat?

Blake got up and went to the liquor cabinet. He found a bottle of Scotch, grabbed a glass and returned to his chair. After pouring a healthy glass of the liquor, he took a large swallow and almost choked. Blake didn't drink often and when he did, he usually drank wine. But the full realization of what a farce his life was, and his ideas of his vivacious little bride, had been too much to face with only a glass or two of wine.

Blake stared into the empty fireplace, drinking Scotch and contemplating the frailties of the human spirit. There must be a rhyme and a reason to human existence, he decided solemnly. *If we go by the rules and play the game fairly, our lives are supposed to work out satisfactorily.* Blake had operated his life on those principles, but now none of them made sense. All he knew was that his most secret dread had become a reality. He had lost Angel. Or rather, he had never had her to lose. She had been a figment of his imagination. He had wanted her to be loyal and truthful, so he attributed those traits to her. Was it her fault that she was incapable of being faithful to him? He hadn't spent much time with her but he had been with her every night, holding her close, loving her, trying to express what he was feeling in every way he knew.

Only he had never been able to find the words. He didn't have the glib French tongue that Jean-Pierre no doubt had developed at an early age.

Blake knew nothing about love and loving. All he knew was the emotion was too painful to be borne.

Foster found Blake asleep on the couch in the library later that night. His shirttail was pulled out of his pants, and one shoe and sock were pulled off. The other foot was still wearing both. Foster shook his head. An empty Scotch bottle lay on its side on the rug by the couch.

Something had certainly created an emotional storm in the Carlyle household. He hoped they would be strong enough to weather it.

Chapter Nine

Blake rolled heavily onto his side and promptly fell off the couch. "What the hell?" he managed to mutter, while he sat up and rubbed his pounding head.

Early-morning light seeped through the chinks in the drapes and he groaned. What was he doing down here?

Feeling an urgent need to answer nature's call he forced himself into a standing position, noticing for the first time that one of his feet was ready to face the day while the other was totally unadorned. Bits and pieces of the evening before drifted back into his conscious mind and Blake suddenly wished for the peace and tranquillity of total amnesia.

He sat down and pulled the other shoe off, put his sock on his bare foot and, picking up both shoes, padded upstairs, down the hall and into his bedroom, where he found his beautiful, seductive, unfaithful wife sound asleep. He dropped his shoes near his closet door, wincing at the ungodly racket they made hitting the plush carpeting. With firm resolve he headed for the shower, determined to do whatever he could to relieve himself of his pain. First, the physical. He searched around for headache tablets, found the bottle and dropped three in the palm of his hand. After washing them down with water he turned on the shower and stepped in, almost buckling under the strong force of the spray.

What the hell did you hope to prove last night, anyway? he asked himself caustically. *Any numskull can crawl into a bottle and drown his troubles, but the problem is he only succeeds in drowning himself. The troubles are still there with the additional pain of a hangover.* Blake's logical mind took delight in pointing out the irrationality of his behavior.

Angel slowly came awake to the sound of water running. She felt disoriented and depressed but couldn't quite discover why. Her head ached and her mouth was so dry she could barely swallow. The sound of water had forced itself on her consciousness to relieve her body's thirst. She rolled over and discovered that Blake's side of the bed was undisturbed. He hadn't come home last night.

The events of the previous day suddenly filled her memory, and Angel gave a soft cry. After he found out she had seen Marcia he must not have felt a need to come home!

But what about the water that was running? Cautiously Angel sat up in bed, holding her head as though afraid it would topple from her shoulders. She felt as though she had a hangover. Hadn't Jean-Pierre given her something to drink? Then later, some sort of capsule to take? She must have mixed something sizable to feel as fragile as she did at the moment.

The water stopped running and Angel realized she had heard the shower. So Blake had finally returned home in time to get ready to go to work.

Debating whether to wait until he came out or go and get a drink of water, her thirst won out and Angel slipped out of bed, noticing for the first time she had slept in her panties and bra. She grabbed her robe and quickly tied it around her waist, then lifting her chin slightly she proceeded into the bathroom.

Blake was drying himself when she walked in, his broad muscular back causing a pang deep inside of her. She loved him so much. That was the very last thing, however, he would want to hear from her.

She walked over to the sink and turned on the cold water. At the sound, Blake glanced around and saw her. They both stared at each other, waiting for the other to speak. Angel studied his face. He looked as though he'd been up most of the night, which was probably the case. His expression was dispassionate.

She had no idea what he was thinking. She never did.

Blake studied his petite wife and wondered how she managed to keep that innocent, fragile appearance. She had certainly had him fooled. Her eyes were huge in her face and faint shadows curved beneath them. She seemed unusually pale and his words surprised both of them.

"Are you feeling all right?"

Was he feeling some remorse? He looked concerned. "I am still feeling tired, for some reason," she admitted.

Blake experienced a sudden clear image of her spending the afternoon in bed with Jean-Pierre. It was so clear it was almost like seeing it on film. "I can imagine," he muttered, tossing his towel in the hamper and striding out of the bathroom like primitive man before the advent of clothing.

She followed him back into the bedroom. He had disappeared into his closet and came out with a suit and shirt. "When did you get home?" She tried to keep her voice low and pleasant, hoping to mask her sense of outrage.

"About four-thirty. You were asleep."

Of course, I'd be asleep at that time of the morning, you idiot! she wanted to scream at him.

Hoping to forestall yet another comment on the unusual time, Blake said, "Before you say anything, I did not come home at that time because I was ill!"

"I'm sure you didn't."

"But you don't have to worry. I won't come home like that again."

What did he expect her to say? Thank you for not spending every night with your mistress? Thank you for coming home to me once in a while?

Angel decided she'd better not comment. No doubt it was safer that way.

"Isn't it a little early to be getting dressed?" she asked, trying to find a neutral subject. She wasn't ready to discuss what she'd learned yesterday with him. She wasn't sure she would ever be able to discuss it.

Blake glanced at his watch. It was almost six o'clock. He generally wasn't up for another hour at least. But he certainly wasn't in the mood to stay around home making innocuous conversation with his cheating wife. Sooner or later he would have to let her know he was aware of her affair, but not today. At least let him get rid of the blasted tom-toms in his head first. Then he would have it out with her. But not now.

"I've got some work to catch up on," he muttered, using the first excuse he could think of.

"I'm sure you have," she said, too soft for him to hear. She wondered how many nights he had been at the office and how many of those nights he'd been with Marcia. There was probably a whole backlog of work piling up waiting for his attention!

"Why don't you go back to bed if you're still tired?"

"What a good idea. I'm surprised I didn't think of it myself." Angel marched back to the bed and crawled under the covers, pulling them up to her chin. "Have a good day," she said, closing her eyes against the way Blake looked in that charcoal-gray suit. It wasn't fair that he should look so wonderful and be such a bastard. But maybe there was a philosophical point to be made out of the correlation between the two. Was it possible that only the good-looking ones could afford to be bastards, thinking their looks would go a long way to gaining them forgiveness? The less than handsome men couldn't afford to take the chance, so tried harder to be trustworthy.

Angel decided she'd have to ponder that one for a while. She might even be able to write a book about her theory someday. Perhaps it would parallel the popularity of *The Cinderella Complex*. It might take a great deal of research but she suspected she could learn an inordinate amount from the bastard she'd married.

For the next several days the Carlyle household appeared normal to any outside observer. Blake came home long after Angel had gone to bed at night and left before she got up, which took care of the necessity of conversation between the two of them. Angel was too heartsick to care. What, after all, was there to say? From her continued sluggishness in the morning she had a hunch that she could very well be pregnant. If that were the case he would no doubt be relieved to know his marital duties were accomplished.

The doctor confirmed her suspicions the day of the preopening presentation of her work by the art gallery.

Blake, as usual, was late getting home. Angel had already eaten and was dressed, waiting for him, when he arrived. It was the first good look she had had of him in a while and she was shocked at his appearance. He looked terrible. His face was drawn; he'd obviously lost weight; his color was pallid. For a moment Angel felt sorry for him, but only for a moment. His double life was catching up with him. She would wait until they returned home tonight and let him know her news. She knew he would find it a relief.

Angel was curled up in Blake's favorite chair in the library when he arrived home the day of her opening. He had been dreading the evening all day. The only way he could be civil to her was to avoid her. Now he had to spend an entire evening with her.

Blake had never asked if she intended to announce that she was the artist known as AB. If she didn't want it known, he certainly wasn't going to be the one to mention it. No wonder she didn't need any money from the sale of the stocks. She would be very comfortable from the sales of her paintings alone.

She stood up when he walked into the room and Blake felt the now familiar pain deep within him whenever he saw her. Angel wore a sheer black gown, Grecian in effect, with one shoulder bare. Her hair was in elaborate coils, giving her a regal appearance. A less heavenly angel he'd never seen. She looked seductive, enticing, and he wanted her so badly he ached with it.

Since the day he had found Jean-Pierre at the house, Blake had deliberately refrained from making love to her. Every time he thought about it he saw her with Jean-Pierre instead, and a gut-wrenching pain shot through him. But he had grown accustomed to her loving nature and he missed her so much. He had to remind himself that he didn't miss the actual person, only the woman he had thought she was. He could get over the real Angel, but it would take time. He wondered if he would ever stop loving the figment of his imagination he had thought was her.

"You look beautiful, Angel. I'll be the envy of every man there tonight when I walk in with you on my arm," he said quietly.

She felt the heat of color rise in her cheeks at his compliment. He sounded so sincere and she suddenly wished things had worked out differently between them.

"Thank you, Blake. I've been so nervous all day.

I appreciate your kind remark." She glanced at the clock on the mantel. "Have you eaten?"

He shook his head. "I didn't want to take the time."

"I'll have Gina get your dinner ready while you change."

"But won't that make you late?"

"It doesn't matter. I don't even need to be there, you know."

"You mean you aren't going to tell anyone who you are?"

"I didn't plan on it. Why?"

"I don't know, really. I just don't see the need for secrecy."

"There really isn't any now. When I first started selling I felt my age and sex would hinder the sale value, but now it really doesn't matter." She looked at him quizzically. "If I were to acknowledge that I am the artist, I'm afraid Marcia might be embarrassed by her earlier remarks."

"I'll try to tell her myself before the general announcement. I'm sure she'll understand. She obviously values your work." He pulled his tie off. "I'll go up and change, then. Tell Gina I'll be down in fifteen minutes."

While waiting for Blake to return downstairs, Angel pondered his unexpected remarks. He hadn't sounded as though he was concerned over Marcia's feelings. It was hard to tell with Blake, though.

Perhaps things would change when he knew that he was going to become a father. From the little they had discussed on their honeymoon, he had given her the impression that he looked forward to their having a child, possibly more than one. Perhaps Jean-Pierre had been right and she had overreacted to Marcia's comments. Perhaps she had given up too soon. After all, Marcia had spent two years with him, Angel barely two months. It might take time to win him away from her, but he was worth fighting for.

A strange sense of peace settled over her, and Angel knew she had made the right decision. She loved Blake and she wanted to make her marriage work. She refused to concede defeat until Blake announced it was over.

When Blake returned downstairs, Angel met him at the bottom of the steps. "You look absolutely gorgeous in formal clothes, are you aware of that?" she asked. "Sinfully so."

He raised an eyebrow at her sudden change of mood. He hadn't seen her so animated in—he couldn't remember when. "I'm glad you approve." He placed her hand on his sleeve and escorted her into the small dining alcove, where his dinner awaited him. She sat across from him, sipping her wine, sharing all the things she had done for the past few years, giving him a running commentary of the tragic-comedic aspects of the art show—the multiple discussions of framing and lighting, of placement, of a hundred different details that someone out of the field would not understand.

Blake could feel himself relaxing and his guard slipping. For a little while he could pretend that they were on their honeymoon once again. When he suddenly burst out laughing at one of her anecdotes Angel realized that was what she had been trying to do—make him laugh. He looked years younger. When had she last heard him sound so lighthearted? His eyes were sparkling and the look of admiration telegraphed a sensuous message to Angel that made her quiver.

There was a large gathering at the gallery when they arrived and Mr. Huntington was wringing his hands. "I was beginning to think you weren't even going to show up," he exclaimed.

"You don't need me now, Henry. My part of it is already accomplished." She tucked her arm tightly around Blake's, her breath brushing against his elbow. "By the way, Henry, this is my husband, Blake Carlyle. Henry Huntington is the owner of the gallery, Blake."

Blake smiled. The nervous man seemed to be near hysteria. "My wife has told me a great deal about you," he said honestly, but wouldn't dare go into much detail about the type of hilarious stories she'd recounted.

Henry stuck out his hand. "Well, it's my pleasure to meet you at last, Mr. Carlyle. I don't mean to be rude, but I really would like to introduce Angel to some of the people here tonight, if you don't mind?"

"Not at all." He raised Angel's hand to his mouth and softly kissed the palm. "Why don't you accept the acclaim that is rightfully yours, darling? You deserve it."

She searched his expression and saw nothing but warm tenderness. Something magical had happened tonight. They had been transported back in time to that first week of marriage, when they were so close and loving and so in tune with each other. This time Angel was determined to hang on to that magic or, at the very least, learn to produce her own.

She grinned—a spontaneous, gamine smile that lit up her face. "You're right, Blake. It's time I face the music." She turned to Henry and nodded regally. "I am ready to meet your patrons, Henry."

Angel and Henry had no sooner walked away than Marcia appeared at Blake's shoulder. She wore a golden gown that was flattering to her coloring, and Blake realized that he no longer felt guilty about her. He loved his wife and he sincerely hoped Marcia would find someone to love, as well. He knew it would never be him.

"Hello, Blake. I wasn't sure if you would be here tonight. Are you alone?" She glanced around the room as though searching for Angel.

"No, Angel is here. I'm glad to see you myself. There's something I've been meaning to tell you."

Marcia's face lit up, obviously waiting for good news.

"I didn't have the opportunity to tell you when you brought the painting over, but despite what your father might have found out, I married Angel because I love her. I did not mean to hurt you, and I'm sincerely sorry I did, but you need to understand the truth about my feelings for her."

Marcia stared at him, stricken. "Oh, Blake. Then her affair with Jean-Pierre must be extremely painful for you."

Blake controlled the flinch he felt at the mention of the Frenchman's name. "Whatever my feelings, they are private and I don't want to discuss them."

"I'm sorry. I wasn't thinking. I was so hoping that you intended to separate as soon as you could. Wishful thinking on part, I suppose."

"There's another thing that Angel wanted me to tell you. She had intended to tell you the night you gave us the painting. You see, Angel is the artist AB. She didn't tell you because she didn't want to embarrass you. And she was concerned how you would take the announcement tonight."

Marcia seemed to wilt before his eyes. "And I gave you one of her paintings? She must have found that amusing."

"No, Marcia. Angel isn't like that. She was only concerned about your feelings."

"Thank you for telling me. If you don't mind, I

don't believe I'll stay for the general announcement."

Blake stood in the crowd and watched Marcia leave the room. Then his attention was drawn to the front by the PA system.

"Ladies and gentlemen! If I may have your attention, please," Henry said over a microphone. When the hubbub of conversation died down, he cleared his throat nervously and said, "I want to welcome you to the gallery tonight on this very special occasion. Not only do we have a group of paintings collected here that we are most privileged to display, but we also have the artist present for a first personal appearance." He glanced around the room with a pleased expression. "The artist known as AB is actually Angel Bennington Carlyle. Her halo signature has been a play on her name, and the name AB, of course, represents the initials of her first and maiden names. We here in San Francisco are very fortunate that Angel met and fell in love with one of our own native sons and is now making her home here with us. Ladies and gentlemen—let's welcome Angel Bennington Carlyle."

"Well, I'll be damned," Jeremy muttered slightly behind Blake.

"More than likely," Blake agreed.

"Did you know?"

"Yes."

"Why didn't you tell someone? Like me, for instance?"

"It wasn't my secret to tell."

"Is that the reason she was spending so much time with that Frenchman?"

Jeremy could have talked all night without reminding Blake of Jean-Pierre Armand. "Could be."

"I'm amazed. I really am. I knew Angel was an artist, but everyone and his mother makes the same claim. It seems to be the in thing these days. But she's a real professional."

"Yes."

"I bet you're really proud of her."

"Very."

"You know, Blake, one of the reasons I admire you so much is your mastery of the English language—such eloquence, such facility of usage! Your virtuosity never ceases to astound me."

"Shut up, Jeremy."

"See what I mean? The right phrase for the right occasion. Have you had any of the champagne yet?"

"No. We just got here."

"Well, let's go celebrate your wife's unqualified success. I promise not to talk."

"I'll drink to that."

The two friends sauntered over to the bar set up near the entrance and got a drink, then wandered through the gallery admiring Angel's artistic genius.

For at least the hundredth time in her life, Angel

wished she were taller. She had lost Blake in the crowd, although she knew he could always spot her—she was surrounded by people. She didn't blame him for refusing to fight the mob. She was beginning to feel a little breathless herself.

"Would it be possible to have a drink of water?" she finally asked Henry.

"Oh, of course, Angel. How about a glass of champagne?"

"I'd much prefer water. It seems so close in here."

"With all these people crowding around you, I'm sure it does." He raised his voice slightly. "If you'll excuse us, please. Angel needs to move along here." He took her arm and led her to the bar, where he had the bartender prepare a large glass with ice and water. She drank from it gratefully.

"You see, there was nothing to be nervous about, was there? They all love you."

Angel glanced up and saw Blake standing beside her. "Oh, Blake, I'm so glad to see you!"

He noted her paleness with concern. "What's wrong?"

"Oh, nothing, but I don't like crowds. They always remind me of lynching parties or something."

"In that case, stick with me, kid. I won't let them get to you again."

"That would be wonderful. A little fame is a wonderful thing. Too much can be a real pain in the—"

"Angel—" Blake drawled, a warning in his low voice.

"You get the general idea."

"Yes."

"Was that a mirage or did I see Jeremy earlier?"

"I wish it was a mirage, but yes, it was Jeremy Jordan in the flesh."

"Why would you prefer a mirage?"

"They're quieter, for one thing." He glanced down at her puzzled expression. "Never mind. Let's go find him. He wants to add his accolade."

The rest of the evening was a blur to Angel and she didn't know what she would have done without Blake to run interference. She wasn't at all sure she was ready to handle the celebrity status her announcement had created for her. She stayed near Blake and felt even more comforted when he drew her within the circle of his arms, keeping her close.

Angel finally admitted her one desire was to escape, and Blake quickly eased her out of the throng without anyone being aware they were departing. Once outside they ran for the car like truant children. They were both laughing by the time they drove away.

The shower felt heavenly to her and she stood in the steady spray without moving, feeling the tight muscles in her neck and shoulders relax. Her eyes had drifted closed and she was almost in a trancelike state when the shower door suddenly opened. Startled, her eyes flew open. Blake stepped inside, carefully closing the door behind him. He took the neglected washcloth from her hand and carefully turned her around. "I thought you might need some help scrubbing your back." He stroked the sudsy cloth along her spine, rubbing gently. Angel felt as though she was receiving tiny electrical shocks everywhere he touched her.

When he finished, Blake turned her around so that she faced him. "Now it's your turn," he said, handing her the cloth.

Numbly, Angel took the cloth and slowly began to rub it across his chest. She refused to meet his eyes. It was obvious from the condition of his body that he hadn't decided to share her shower just to conserve water.

He chuckled when her hand hesitated at his abdomen and obligingly turned around so she could scrub his back. It seemed like weeks since Angel had touched him, and she enjoyed feeling the muscles ripple just below his skin wherever she touched him.

Blake turned to face her once more, rinsing the soap off his body. Then he turned off the water. After opening the shower door, he scooped her up in his arms and carried her into the bedroom. "Blake, we're dripping water everywhere."

"Who cares?" he murmured, his mouth finding hers.

After a few moments, Angel managed to find her breath. "Not me."

He threw the covers back with one hand, then lowered her to the center of the bed. "You are so beautiful," he said softly.

"So are you," she sighed, stroking her hands across his chest and shoulders.

"God, I hope not! Being beautiful would have to be at the top of my list of things I'd prefer not to be."

"Handsome, then."

"I'll accept that."

"You are, Blake. I think you are one of the best-looking, best-built men I know."

"It's obvious you don't know many, then, but I'd just as soon keep it that way." He took the top sheet and blotted her dry, turning her over so that he could remove any moisture left there, but most of it was gone. She knew her body heat must have caused instant evaporation.

It had been so long since he had made love to her, and she wanted him so much. She wanted to let him know how much and began kissing him—light, darting kisses—across his neck and chest. Her lips brushed against his nipples and she felt them contract at her touch. She smiled, pleased at the reaction.

They seemed to come together in an explosion of feeling. Blake held her so tightly she could scarcely draw breath, and his urgent kisses turned her into a flame. She loved him aggressively for the first time, initiating touches and kisses, showing him that as her teacher he had taught her well. When he possessed her she thought she would faint with the joy of it and she responded to him with every atom of her being.

Eventually they fell asleep, exhausted, but later Angel was awakened—again and again—with Blake stroking her, kissing her everywhere, worshiping her with his body.

She tried to respond in a similar fashion but often was carried away with what he was doing to her. He taught her to acknowledge her own loving nature and not to be afraid to show her response to him. And he taught her, finally and irrevocably, that there would never be another man for her.

Chapter Ten

Angel woke up the next morning feeling that all was right with her world. She had made the plunge and disclosed her identity to the art world and nothing dire had happened to her. She had also made up her mind to fight for her marriage, and the difference in their relationship was already apparent.

Blake had not left early that morning. As a matter of fact, she was very aware of him because her back was snuggled up to his chest so that his warmth touched her from her head to her toes. Her cheek rested partially on her pillow and partially on his arm that lay underneath her. His other arm was securely tucked around her waist, his hand resting lightly on her breast.

Once again the days of their honeymoon drifted

through her mind and she smiled. Maybe her aggressiveness last night was what had been lacking in their relationship. Being inexperienced, she wasn't sure how much to participate in their lovemaking and had always allowed Blake to take the lead. But last night she had felt freed from their past, almost renewed with her determination to make the relationship work.

Angel wriggled, attempting to stretch, and Blake's hold on her waist tightened.

"Where do you think you're going?" he said in a gruff, early-morning voice.

She relaxed against him once again, turning her head slightly. "Nowhere. I was just trying to stretch."

"Well, in that case—" He rolled onto his back, straightening his legs and carefully pulling his arm from under her head with a muffled groan.

Angel sat up, raising her arms high above her head, then dropped them and slithered back down along his side, her chin resting on his chest.

"Good morning."

Blake opened one eye and glanced at her, then closed it, a smile forming on his lips. "It certainly seems to be."

"Aren't you going to be late for work?"

"Probably."

"Is it going to cause a problem for you?"

"I doubt that anyone would fire me."

She chuckled. "Good point."

He brought his hand up from behind her back and began to stroke her hair. "Did you sleep all right?"

"I have no idea. Someone kept waking me up all night."

"Have any idea who?"

"I was too sleepy to get a good look at him. But I'd recognize his body in the dark anywhere."

Blake pulled her onto his chest and began to kiss her—slow, lazy kisses that caused her muscles and bones to turn into soft wax. She responded wholeheartedly. Eventually she lay on top of him, her body stretched the length of his. From her newfound position Angel discovered how well they fit together and with very little adjusting was able to engage Blake in some serious lovemaking.

She lost track of time. It no longer mattered. Blake was there with her, loving her, and her world was a perfect place.

Sometime later they lay in a tangle of sheets, their bodies covered with a glistening sheen of perspiration, when Angel decided that it was time to share her happy news.

"Blake?" she murmured.

"Hmm?" He sounded almost asleep.

"I have some news for you."

"If you're going to tell me that you're an insatiable hussy, I've already managed to get the message."

She almost choked on sudden laughter. "Sorry. That wasn't it."

"I'm not sure I can take any more."

"Oh, I think you'll like this news."

He sighed. Blake hadn't felt so relaxed in months. Not since their honeymoon, in fact. He had carefully kept his mind blank since he had arrived home last night and found her waiting for him. He prayed that he could continue to control his thoughts and emotions.

They still lay together, their legs intertwined, with her head resting on his chest. He opened his eyes lazily and stared down at her bright blue ones.

"So tell me."

"I'm pregnant," she said in a lilting voice with a mischievous grin.

She felt Blake go rigid and he suddenly sat up as though recoiling from her.

"You're what?"

She laughed uncertainly. "You needn't act so shocked, Blake. You have done an outstanding job since we married to make sure the event took place as soon as possible. I thought you might like to know that all of your efforts were not in vain." She watched him in amazement, bewildered by the instant change from the relaxed, well-loved male she had so recently enjoyed into the hard-faced, cold and aloof stranger he could become with seeming ease.

With her words, Blake was dumped out of his

warm, sensuous haze into the cold reality of morning. Angel was pregnant.

Jean-Pierre! She had never admitted her affair with the Frenchman. Instead, she was going to allow Blake to think the baby was unquestionably his.

When had she decided not to take the chance that she and Blake might not produce a child soon enough to suit her? Was she so eager to return to France that she hadn't wanted to wait even a few months more?

"I thought you'd be happy."

Blake sat up on the side of the bed, running his hands through his hair in an attempt to get it out of his face. She sounded so hurt, like a little girl, all sweetness and innocence. Innocent! That was almost enough to make him laugh. Her lovemaking had been anything but innocent last night. If there had ever been a doubt in his mind regarding her relationship with Jean-Pierre, her behavior in bed last night had convinced him she had been busy learning some intricate skills in how to drive a man out of his head with wanting her. She had been fiery—almost aggressive—and he had been too wrapped up in the sensations she was provoking to take time to examine how she could have learned so much.

He had known. But for a few hours—last night and this morning—he had pushed that knowledge far back into his head, hoping not to have to face it.

However, he wasn't such an idiot that he would perpetually close his mind and heart to what she had done. Facts were facts. How he felt about them was no longer important.

"Why should I be happy?" he finally answered.

He rose from the bed and strode into the bathroom, reaching into the shower and turning on the water full force.

Angel continued to sit on the bed, stunned at the sudden change in his mood. What in the world was wrong? A person would think he had never wanted children or something. It didn't make any sense. The whole purpose of their marriage was for her to have at least one child.

Why should the news upset him now?

She scooted to the edge of the bed and stood up, uncertain what to do next. When she finally forced herself to walk into the bathroom, Blake was stepping out of the shower. He reached past her shoulder for a towel, refusing to look at her. His face looked stern and harsh.

Turning the shower back on, Angel quickly soaped down and rinsed, then got out. She patted herself dry with a towel and pulled her robe off a hook behind the door.

Blake was shaving and she sat down on the vanity stool nearby.

"I seem to be missing something," she said. "But wasn't the purpose of this marriage to produce a child?"

"It certainly was. And you get to go to the top of

the class for innovative techniques to assure you got pregnant as soon as possible.''

''I don't have the faintest idea what you're talking about.''

Blake switched off his electric razor and turned to her. ''Then I'll explain it to you in words of one syllable. In order to make sure you became pregnant immediately you enlisted the help of two, not just one, willing males to double your exposure, so to speak, to the condition.'' He picked up a comb and began to smooth his hair. ''It's really unfortunate that neither Jean-Pierre nor I will ever know for sure which one of us has become a proud father, but since it will carry my name, I have the privilege of claiming what may very well turn out to be Jean-Pierre's child!''

A sudden surge of nausea and dizziness swept over Angel and she thought for a moment she was going to faint. Blake threw the comb down and walked out of the room. She barely had the strength to close and lock the door before she was violently ill, her pain and agony as much emotional as physical.

Vaguely she heard a tap on the door and Blake's voice. ''Angel, are you all right?'' There was even a hint of concern. Nice touch, that.

Angel knelt in front of the toilet and when she felt that she had lost all of her insides she sank down to the wonderfully cool tile floor. If she could only rest for a few moments, she would be all right. She stretched out along the floor, her cheek resting against the soothing tile.

Blake found her lying on the floor when he got the door open. She was ghastly white, her hair looking like a wig around her ashen face.

"Angel?"

She didn't answer him and he didn't know if she was asleep or unconscious. It had taken him forever to find the damned key to the bathroom. They never locked the door and he hadn't ever needed it before.

She had not moved and it scared him. He wished he knew who her doctor was. He hadn't thought to ask. Blake didn't even know how far along she was. They had barely been married six weeks.

So if she is at least six weeks pregnant, there wouldn't be any doubt the baby is yours. You know she hadn't been with another man before you married her. Wouldn't it be the height of irony if she had discovered she needn't have worried about getting pregnant, that their first week together had sufficed?

But maybe she did know. Perhaps she felt that once she was pregnant she was free to enjoy her life in her own way and that she no longer owed Blake anything. She had fulfilled her part of the bargain.

Blake wondered how soon a woman could tell she was pregnant. He knew so little about those things. He glanced down at the woman in his arms. She was so tiny and looked so wan and lost somehow. Gently he laid her on the bed and pulled the covers up around her neck. Then he went in search of Foster.

"Angel is sick," he stated baldly.

The older man was all concern. "Shall I call the doctor, sir?"

"I don't know who she's seeing. This may be just morning sickness. She's going to have a baby."

"Congratulations, sir."

"Thank you. The thing is, she needs to eat something. Maybe some tea and toast. Would you have some made up for her?"

"Certainly, sir."

Blake searched through the desk in the library, hoping to find a name or phone number, but nothing turned up. He hated to awaken her to find out, but he supposed that was the quickest way.

Angel lay where he'd placed her a short time ago, but now her eyes were open. They looked bruised, with dark circles beneath them.

Blake walked over to the bed. "How do you feel?"

She moved her head restlessly on the pillow. "I'm all right."

"I'm sure you are, but I think we should call the doctor just the same. Who did you go see?"

"Dr. Friedrichs."

"I'll call him."

"No. Please don't. I'll be all right. He said I might have a few disagreeable symptoms."

"Foster is going to bring you some tea and toast. Maybe that will help."

She nodded.

"Do you want me to stay with you?"

She shook her head quickly and closed her eyes, but not before large tears slipped down her cheeks.

"Don't cry, Angel, please." He took her hand and he felt it go rigid at his touch. "Look, we'll work something out between us. You just get to feeling better. We'll sit down together tonight and talk about the situation. I'll be home early." He let go of her hand and she quickly tucked it under the covers. She kept her eyes closed.

He leaned down and kissed her on the cheek. She flinched.

"Please don't cry."

She lay there quietly listening, waiting for his footsteps to reassure her that he had left the room. Angel remained tense, praying he would go, hoping that she never had to see him again.

When she had opened her eyes and recalled his reaction to her news, all the queasiness returned to her stomach. Did he honestly believe that she had been to bed with Jean-Pierre, or was that his way of justifying his behavior with Marcia to himself? She would probably never know. It no longer mattered.

There was a tap on the door and she opened her eyes. She was alone. "Come in."

Foster opened the door, casually balancing a small

tray. He gave her an uncharacteristic smile, warm and affectionate. "I understand congratulations are in order, Mrs. Carlyle. I couldn't be more pleased. This house has needed to be filled with a family." He set the tray down on the table by the bed. "Gina made you some toast and tea. Try to eat and drink as much of it as you can. I understand that keeping something in your stomach helps alleviate early-morning nausea. If you'd like, I could have some brought up early each morning so it would be waiting for you when you awake."

Angel slowly pushed herself up in bed. She was still wearing her robe, thank goodness. Foster quickly stuffed another pillow behind her head. "We'll see, Foster. Thank you for your consideration."

"It's my pleasure, Mrs. Carlyle. You've added such a sparkle of light and color to our lives. Mr. Blake is a different person since you came."

Is he? What sort of person would automatically assume that if his wife is pregnant, it couldn't be his child? A rather small-minded, suspicious person, Angel wanted to point out. He hadn't even asked her if his suspicions were true. She had been judged without a jury, without knowing of the evidence against her, and found guilty.

Angel carefully consumed the toast and tea, willing her stomach to settle down and behave itself. She had a great deal to accomplish in a very short time. A well-behaved stomach was a must.

Hours later Angel was comfortably ensconced in the first-class section of a jumbo jet on her way to France.

She had called Jean-Pierre and explained to him that she was returning to their home but had not told him why. He didn't need to know of Blake's ridiculous accusations and she was afraid it might affect their friendship. Jean-Pierre might even wonder if she had used him in some way to make Blake jealous.

That was almost funny. Blake jealous? First, you had to have feelings. That man had none.

After that she had called the airlines and asked for the first available flight out of San Francisco, going in any direction. She had been fortunate to find one with connecting flights to Europe.

Angel hadn't bothered packing more than a small case that she could carry with her. Clothes were the least of her concern at the moment. She would be needing a whole new wardrobe in the coming months, anyway. According to Dr. Friedrichs she must have gotten pregnant on her wedding night! He predicted the baby's birth to be sometime in late January.

The last thing Angel had done before she left was to leave a note for Blake. He had said he would be home early to talk. Now there was no reason to go through the sham of discussing their future plans. She didn't feel that she could ever see the man again without reexperiencing that horrible moment of pain when he had accused her of not even knowing for sure who had fathered her baby.

Blake spent his day in the seclusion of his office. He had told Phyllis to hold his calls and cancel his appointments. Whenever Blake had been faced with a problem in the past he had taken the time to examine it from every angle, look at his options and make a rational decision based on all the facts.

The most obvious fact to face at the moment was Angel's pregnancy. Pushing all the annoying emotions away, that fact took precedence over everything else. Their mission was accomplished. They were going to have a child. The stocks were safe.

The second fact that Blake felt to be important was that he loved Angel and wanted to have a strong, meaningful relationship with her. In order to accomplish that goal, he would need to discover if her attachment to Jean-Pierre could ever be severed. Blake knew he would never be able to share her.

Therefore, when he got home that night he would have to ask her to declare her feelings—both for him and for Jean-Pierre.

Perhaps it would help if he first told her how he felt about her? But no. What if that would inhibit her from being completely honest with him? If she didn't love him, he didn't want to keep her in the marriage. Blake refused to face what he would feel if she did not love him. He would just have to accept it, that's all.

With a course of action in mind, he was able to relax somewhat and think about the idea of becoming a father. He would treat the child as though it were his, no matter what. The innocent child need never know the possible truth. He tried to picture a baby girl or boy—red hair, perhaps? Maybe black, like his? He hoped he wouldn't be faced with brown curls.

Blake suddenly remembered what Angel had looked like when she was an infant. He had never seen anything more perfect in his life. Lydia and Yvette had allowed the six-year-old Blake to hold her, and he had sat there perfectly still, staring down into the wide blue eyes that had stared back up at him in fascination.

He suddenly hoped the baby was a girl and that she looked just like her mother. Blake couldn't think of anything he had ever wanted more in his life. Another Angel to love. Even if Angel chose Jean-Pierre, the baby would legally be Blake's. No wonder Scott had become such a doting father. Blake had a hunch he would be the same.

He leaned back in his chair, a slight smile on his face, daydreaming about a future that included a loving wife and several children—and no Frenchman hovering in the background.

* * *

Blake arrived at home at five, eager to see Angel. He had called at lunchtime to see how she was feeling and Foster had informed him she was resting. He was glad to hear it.

He glanced in the library but the room was empty. He had started up the stairs when Foster appeared in the foyer. "Is Angel still upstairs?"

"No, sir. She isn't here."

Blake paused, one foot slowly coming down on the next highest step. "Where is she?"

"I don't know, sir. She said to tell you she left you a message on the desk in the library."

A cold hand clutched at his heart and Blake shivered. He didn't like the sound of things. The one constant in all of his plans was that Angel would be there to talk to him. He turned around and went downstairs again.

Flipping on the switch of the desk lamp, Blake sat down in the chair and slowly reached for the envelope with his name written across the front. The envelope was sealed.

He pulled out the sheets of paper with sudden dread.

Dear Blake,

By the time you read this I will be on my way home to France. I believe the original agreement between the two of us has now been fulfilled. According to the doctor, the baby is due in late January. I will let you know when the baby arrives so that the legal papers can be prepared, but for all practical purposes you now have control of the company.

I hope that you and Marcia will be able to continue your relationship unhampered by your need to come home now. I will sign any papers you wish in order to terminate the marriage at the proper time. I am sure Harry will know how to handle everything.

Wishing you the best in the future.
Angel

Blake stared numbly at the sheets of paper in his hand. If the baby was due in January, then it had to be his. What was she talking about? Marcia wasn't a part of his life. Angel would know that better than anyone. He had scarcely had time to spend with her, much less the energy for anyone else.

She hadn't mentioned a word about Jean-Pierre. Had he gone home with her? Did it matter at this point? Angel wanted her freedom from him. He hadn't needed to sit down and talk with her. She had given him the answers to several of his questions.

Perhaps it was better this way. Blake recognized he wasn't husband material. Even Jeremy had pointed that out to him. He didn't share his feelings enough. He didn't know how to let down his guard with people. He had begun to relax with Angel but it hadn't been enough, obviously. Of course, it would have been different if she had married him out of love, rather than a sense of obligation.

He wondered how his dad and Scott had ever hoped that he and Angel would be able to have a working relationship together. She deserved so much more than he could give her. She needed to be around people like Jean-Pierre, uncomplicated people who were not afraid of being hurt, who were willing to give of themselves.

The only thing Blake knew anything about was the corporate business world. It was better if he stuck with what he knew.

Making that decision did not seem to ease the pain in his chest. He realized he had been holding his breath for long moments, letting go only when the lack of oxygen was too painful. Now he forced himself to take several deep breaths, forced himself to relax. Of course there was going to be a certain amount of pain to work through. He wondered why people seemed so enthusiastic about their emotions. They had caused so much pain for him he would willingly do without them for the rest of his life.

Blake walked over to the bar and picked up a bottle of Scotch and a glass. He remembered his dad, Harry and Scott celebrating various successes with a round of drinking that would have killed ordinary men. It was funny; he never thought about drinking when he was pleased about an accomplishment.

Blake used the liquor to blank out his mind for a little while, to give him a chance to adjust to things. As a matter of fact, it was only since Angel had come into his life that he had felt the need for an alcoholic oblivion.

He carefully poured a glass of Scotch and slowly took a sip. Not bad, once you got used to the initial taste. Well, since Angel was no longer in his life, he probably wouldn't need to drink, so he might as well enjoy the smooth Scotch at the moment.

Blake settled back onto the couch with a sigh. He made a toast to himself. "Congratulations, Blake, old buddy. You're going to become a father." The words echoed in the room, then the silence descended once more.

Chapter Eleven

Summer passed and autumn soon followed. Angel was reabsorbed into her circle of friends and at times felt that she had only imagined her few short months in San Francisco. Only the growing evidence of the child she carried reminded her that she and Blake were going to become parents.

She hadn't heard from Blake since she left, but then she hadn't expected him to respond to her letter. What was there for him to say? She had given him everything he wanted, including his freedom. Since she hadn't heard anything about a divorce, she assumed he and Harry had decided to wait until after the baby was born. After all, there was no hurry. Now that she was gone, he and Marcia could see each other at any time.

Jean-Pierre had returned to France with commissions for several sculptures. He and Henry Huntington had come to a tentative agreement regarding a show for him in another year or two. With that sort of encouragement, Jean-Pierre and Michelle had laughingly agreed to marry, which in reality meant that she stayed with him all the time, rather than most of the time.

It also meant that Suzanne and Angel needed another roommate. But when they talked about it, Angel admitted that she would probably not stay there after the baby was born.

"I would prefer to stay with my friends until after I have my baby, but this is no place to raise a child. I am going to begin looking for a small cottage somewhere in the countryside so the baby will have some fresh air and sunshine and room to run and play."

Jean-Pierre, Michelle and Suzanne sat around the large loft and listened to Angel's plans with varying degrees of dismay. She sounded so serene, as though it was perfectly normal to be preparing to raise the child on her own, when she had a husband who should certainly be showing some interest.

Jean-Pierre, especially, was more concerned than he would admit to the other women. Angel was not eating enough. As the baby grew she became thinner in other areas. He continued to nag her about eating and insisted on accompanying her on her next visit to the doctor to be sure she was healthy.

The news he received alarmed him even further but he kept it to himself for the moment. Something needed to be done. Angel was pining away for that jackass of a husband and he didn't even care enough to stay in touch. Jean-Pierre waited and watched and when Blake made no attempt even to acknowledge Christmas, Jean-Pierre decided to step in and give the man his opinion of his worth both as a man and as a human being.

Blake was having an unusually hectic day on the Tuesday after the holidays. All hell had broken loose at one of their supplier's plants, and production had been slowed for his company, as well.

He hated the holiday season, anyway. Holidays were not meant to be spent alone. Last year he and his dad had spent an unusually close day together, sharing their views of the company and where it was headed. Todd had brought up the desire to have some grandchildren and Blake had laughed at him, saying there was plenty of time to become a grandfather.

Only there hadn't been. For the first time Blake realized that Todd's grandchild would be born within weeks of the first anniversary of Todd's death. Blake felt a faint shiver course through him. Had Todd lived, there would have been no grandchild.

Blake shook his head, trying to clear the images in his head. He had been haunted by Angel for months. He had discovered that he could no longer sleep in their bedroom. He would wake up each night, reaching for her, and when he remembered she was no longer there he would lie there for hours, picturing her with him, seeing her as she had been with him there.

Eventually he had told Foster to move his belongings down the hall to the corner bedroom. It was smaller but all he needed. And it wasn't haunted by memories of his beautiful wife.

The phone rang at his elbow. He pushed the intercom button. "Yes, Phyllis?"

"You have a transatlantic call, Blake. A Mr. Jean-Pierre Armand is calling."

Blake stared at the innocent black intercom as though it had suddenly turned into a hissing, poisonous snake.

"Can you take the call, Blake?"

Sure, why not? He could also slit his wrists, commit hara-kiri or pour gasoline all over his body and strike a match, but none of them sounded particularly appealing.

Were they already getting so anxious they didn't want to wait until after the birth of the baby to contact him?

He forced himself to reach for the phone. "Yeah, I'll take it." He picked up the instrument and spoke. "Yes, Jean-Pierre?"

"I wondered if you would take the call," was the sardonic response.

"I took it. What do you want?"

"I just wondered if you were the cold-blooded bastard I thought you were or whether you might want to know how Angel is doing."

"Is she all right?"

"At least you gave the correct response. What I need to know is do you care?"

"Of course I care. But cut the word games and tell me why you called?"

"I called to inform you that there's a very good chance that Angel won't survive giving birth to your child. Just thought you'd want to know."

Blake felt as though all the blood in his head drained out and left him light-headed. "What are you talking about?"

"I'm talking about the fact that Angel hasn't been taking proper care of herself, she hasn't gained enough weight and the doctor thinks the baby is going to be large. Whenever he tries to discuss the matter with her, she insists it doesn't matter what happens to her but that the baby *must* live. She told me that since the only thing you ever wanted from her was that baby, she would give it to you, even if she died trying. The point is she very well may."

"Oh, my God." Blake stared at the wall in front of his desk in shocked disbelief. "Do you think she would see me if I came over there?"

"That depends on whether you bring your mistress with you."

"What are you talking about?"

"Your precious Marcia. I really think you two deserve each other. Neither one of you cares how you hurt other people."

"Jean-Pierre, I don't know what you're talking about. I haven't had anything to do with Marcia Sinclair since Angel and I announced our engagement."

"Then why did Miss Sinclair imply that the two of you were merely biding your time, waiting for Angel to return to France?"

"When in the world did she say that?"

"You remember. The day I had to take Angel home because she was hysterical to find out that you were not interested in making your marriage work. That you had continued to spend your evenings with Marcia, letting Angel think you were working. Why else did you think I was upstairs with her, trying to calm her down?"

Blake heard his own voice as though in a distance, his words slowly spaced. "I thought you were having an affair with Angel."

"You what? Why, you stupid bastard. Even if I ever thought of Angel in that way, which I haven't, she couldn't see anybody but you. She fell for you so hard she could scarcely wait to return to San Francisco and marry you."

Blake ignored the rest and latched on to his last words. "Angel loves me?"

"Of course she loves you. Why else do you suppose she's risking her life to have your baby? She knew you only married her to fulfill those ridiculous stipulations that your fathers made. Well, I hope everyone is happy now. They got their marriage, you managed to get her pregnant immediately after the wedding, and all Angel has to do is produce this multimillion-dollar child."

Blake felt as though he was in the middle of a nightmare. Nothing made sense. Angel loved him? She had loved him when they married? She had loved him and had left him?

"I can't believe this."

"Believe it."

"I swear to you that there is absolutely nothing between Marcia and me. I don't care what Angel thought."

"Can I believe that?"

"You damned well can. Jean-Pierre, I have been eaten up with jealousy for months, thinking Angel preferred you."

The background sounds of the transatlantic call were the only response to Blake's explanations. Eventually he heard Jean-Pierre's groan. "What a mix-up. Tell me something, Blake. Did you and Angel at any time ever sit down and talk? I have never heard such a story of misunderstanding and conjectures in my life. It seems to me that most of the activity in the family was both of you jumping to conclusions—invariably the wrong ones!"

"That's a fairly accurate account, I'm afraid. As

a matter of fact, I had come home early the day I met you in the hallway so that we *could* have an opportunity to sit down and discuss things. That's when I felt like part of one of those ridiculous farces about the husband coming home early and finding a man coming out his wife's bedroom. And your comment didn't help any."

"What comment?"

"That you were taking care of my wife since I obviously had other priorities. I thought you were making a dig about the fact that I was so seldom home."

"Hell, no. I was talking about comforting her. She was absolutely flattened when she discovered you had told Marcia the true circumstances surrounding your marriage."

"But I didn't tell Marcia anything about us!"

"You should be telling Angel all of this, not me."

"God, I know. Look, let me see what I can do. Will you give me a number where I can reach you? As soon as I can get a flight verified I'll call you back." He paused, uncertain. "Would you mind meeting me at the airport?"

"Not at all. However, I don't intend to tell Angel you are coming. It will only needlessly upset her."

"You think she'll be upset to see me?"

"She will wonder why you are coming, and since it is not my place to tell her, I would prefer your arrival to come as a surprise."

"Whatever you say. I'll be in touch shortly."

Angel gave up all pretense of trying to paint. Her back had been hurting her since she woke up that morning. The doctor said she still had four more weeks to go before the baby was due but she wondered if her baby had checked the calendar lately.

She couldn't find a comfortable position. She tried sitting, lying and walking, but nothing seemed to help. Angel wondered if she should call the doctor.

There was a tap on the door and she turned, glad to have some company. Suzanne had left several hours ago and Angel didn't know when to expect her. "Come in."

The door opened and Jean-Pierre walked in. "Good morning, Angel. How are you feeling this morning?"

"Pregnant. Why must you ask me that every time you see me?" she grumbled.

He laughed. "I have brought someone to see you," he said, stepping away from the doorway.

Angel had been making her slow way across the loft and was only a few feet away when Blake appeared in the doorway.

"Blake!" She felt her knees begin to shake and she edged over to a chair and sank down into it. He looked tired, as though he hadn't gotten much sleep lately, but other than that he looked marvelous to her.

"Hello, Angel." He came over to her chair and

knelt down on one knee before her. Brushing back wisps of hair from her face, he studied her carefully. She looked pale, but part of that was her normal translucent complexion. Her face and arms looked thinner and the tentlike top she wore did little to camouflage her tummy. He pulled her into his arms gently, holding her against him. They stayed that way, neither noticing that Jean-Pierre had left the room.

"Oh, Angel, will you ever forgive me for allowing you to leave?"

"As I recall," she tried to say shakily, "you didn't have much choice in the matter."

"But I could have been on the next flight over here."

She pulled back from him slightly and looked at him, perplexed. "Why would you have done that?"

"Because I love you so much and it has been agony for me to be away from you."

"You love me?" she repeated faintly.

"Very much."

"But what about—"

"Darling, there's so much to explain. Do you suppose we could find somewhere a little more comfortable to have this discussion?"

She glanced down at him and recognized how awkward his position must be. Pulling herself up from the chair by the simple expedient of using the back of the cane-backed chair as leverage, she led him over to the long sofa pushed against the wall.

"Please understand that if I ever get down, I may never get up again," she said with a slight smile.

Blake sat down beside her and pulled her comfortably back into his arms. He never wanted her more than a few inches away from him again.

"I owe you so many apologies I don't know where to start. I've made such a mess of things from the very beginning. I didn't even recognize that I loved you when we got married. Jeremy had to point that out to me," he said, obviously disgusted.

"It's hard for me to believe."

"I know. I also found out that Marcia made some remarks that upset you. I realize now that nothing she could have said would have bothered you if I'd had the guts to tell you how I felt, but I didn't know how to put my feelings into words." He was quiet for a moment. "As a matter of fact, I still don't."

"You seem to be doing an excellent job at the moment. Don't quit now."

"I'm sorry I ever thought there was something between you and Jean-Pierre, but when I found him coming out of our bedroom that day, I'm afraid I jumped to all of the wrong conclusions."

"You found Jean-Pierre coming out of *our* bedroom? But that's impossible."

"No. It was the day you saw Marcia and were so

upset. He just recently explained to me that he stayed with you until you fell asleep."

Angel thought back for a moment. "But that was the night you never came home."

"Angel. I have never stayed away from you, not ever. I was home every single night we were married."

"But you hadn't been to bed and when I asked when you came home you said four-thirty."

"And you thought I meant in the morning? Oh, darling, what a crazy mix-up. I'm afraid I spent the night on the couch in the library after having consumed an inordinate amount of Scotch."

"But, Blake, you don't drink Scotch."

"You can say that again. I have sworn off the stuff. It almost killed me."

They sat there in comfortable silence, thinking about all that had happened between them. For the first time, they recognized that they had loved each other at the time of the marriage.

Blake echoed her thoughts. "You were such a beautiful bride and I felt so fortunate to be marrying you."

"And I was convinced you were eager to hang on to control of the company."

"I want you in my life, but I also felt a real responsibility to keep the company going, which was why I was putting in those hellishly long hours."

"That I thought were spent with Marcia."

"If I'd only known."

"If *I'd* only known you thought there was something going on between Jean-Pierre and me. I was so shocked when you accused me of not knowing who had fathered my baby."

Blake groaned. "I can't believe how stupid I've been, my love."

"I like the sound of that. 'My love.' I had so much hoped someday that you would love me."

"I've never stopped.' He kissed her, his hand resting on her protruding stomach. He felt a tenseness under his hand that pulled, then slowly let go. He raised his head. "What was that?" He stared down at her rounded middle.

"I'm not sure, but I have a feeling that this baby of ours is getting ready to be born within the next few hours."

"But it can't. You have at least another month to go."

"Fine. Why don't you explain that to your offspring while I call the doctor?" She pushed herself up and went to the phone.

"But, Angel, Jean-Pierre says you're too small to have a baby. That it's dangerous for you."

She picked up the phone and dialed. Without looking around she said, "Jean-Pierre has a big mouth."

"Thank God. If he hadn't called to tell me, I'd still be sitting in San Francisco, thinking you could hardly wait to be free of me."

She glanced over her shoulder. "Is that what you thought?"

He nodded as she began to speak into the phone. He didn't understand her explanations—his French wasn't that good—but he could tell she didn't like the response she was getting. When she finally hung up the phone, she sighed in disgust.

"They want me to meet the doctor at the hospital. He wants to check me."

"Where is it? How do we get there?" He began pacing the floor.

"It's too early to pace, Blake, but if you want to get some practice, go right ahead. Meanwhile, I'll see if Jean-Pierre or Michelle is home. Did he tell you they were married last July?"

"No, as a matter of fact, he didn't mention it."

"Probably didn't think it mattered."

"It would have mattered a great deal to me, if anyone had thought to inform me."

Within minutes her friends arrived and whisked Angel off to the hospital. The doctor agreed that, regardless of their calculations, the baby was on its way.

Blake panicked. He took the doctor aside and explained that he was Angel's husband and that nothing was to stop the doctor from saving her, no matter what happened. The doctor patiently listened without interruption. When Blake ran down, the doctor patted him on the shoulder. "I have every intention of saving them both, *monsieur*. Because of its early arrival, the baby will be less of a threat to Angel because it will be smaller than we anticipated. Just try to stay calm, if that is possible." The doctor grinned reassuringly and left them.

The following hours dragged on for days, or so it seemed to Blake. Michelle and Jean-Pierre, and later Suzanne, attempted to distract him with funny stories of Angel during the past several months, knowing that he calmed down only when he could either talk about her or listen to others talk about her.

It was almost three o'clock in the morning before the doctor reappeared. "You have a beautiful daughter, Monsieur Carlyle. She is barely five pounds but quite healthy, with an excellent set of lungs. If you listen closely, you can hear her from here!"

Blake had come to his feet when the doctor walked into the room, but the news weakened his legs and he sat down again. "A girl."

"Yes," the doctor agreed. "With fuzzy red hair and a ferocious frown. Hopefully she will grow to like her new world shortly."

Blake stood up again. "When may I see Angel?"

"In a few moments. They are taking her to her room at the moment."

"Was it bad for her?"

"Not as much as I had feared. She was much more relaxed and happy than I have seen her in months. I'm sure it helped that you were with her."

"I hope so. I've caused her so much grief."

"But such is life, *monsieur*. Life will always have its ups and downs, but it is what we make of them that is so important."

Blake nodded, his thoughts already with Angel. Jean-Pierre walked over and stuck out his hand. "Congratulations, Blake. I couldn't be happier for you."

"Thanks. I want you to know how much I appreciate all you've done, Jean-Pierre."

"I did it for Angel, Blake. I'm just pleased that everything has worked out so well. I have to admit that I didn't expect to discover that I might even grow to like you."

"Same here."

The men grinned at each other.

A nurse appeared in the doorway. "You may see Madame Carlyle now, if you wish."

Blake followed her down the hallway and into a small private room. Angel was in bed, her stomach considerably flatter than it had been the last time he saw her. Her eyes were closed.

He walked over to the bed and picked up her hand. It was warm and he gripped it, sudden tears flooding his eyes. He loved her so much. What would he have done if he had lost her?

Her eyes flicked open, the shaded light casting shadows over them both.

"Have you seen her?"

"Not yet."

"She looks just like you in a temper," she whispered with a slight smile.

"But she has your hair."

"Oh, yes. My hair and your temper, what a lethal combination!" Angel saw the trace of tears on his cheeks. "What's wrong, my love?"

"Nothing is wrong. Everything is perfect. As soon as you can travel, I'd like to take you home with me."

"I'd like that."

"You'd better get some rest. I'll see you later." He leaned over and kissed her softly.

"Blake?"

"Yes, love?"

"Since our daughter is obviously going to be the chairman of the board, don't you think we should consider producing a president?"

He smiled. "We could certainly give the idea some thought."

"Then, of course," she mused in a sleepy voice, "we'll need officers and a board of directors and—"

"I love you, Angel."

She smiled, a warm, loving glow that radiated throughout the room. "You certainly have a way with words, Blake."

SPECIAL EDITION

Stories of love and life, these powerful novels are tales that you can identify with—romances with "something special" added in!

Fall in love with the stories of authors such as **Nora Roberts, Diana Palmer, Ginna Gray** and many more of your special favorites—as well as wonderful new voices!

Special Edition brings you entertainment for the heart!

SSE-GEN

Do you want...

Dangerously handsome heroes

Evocative, everlasting love stories

Sizzling and tantalizing sensuality

Incredibly sexy miniseries like **MAN OF THE MONTH**

Red-hot romance

Enticing entertainment that can't be beat!

You'll find all of this, and much *more* each and every month in **SILHOUETTE DESIRE**. Don't miss these unforgettable love stories by some of romance's hottest authors. Silhouette Desire—where your fantasies will always come true....

DES-GEN

If you've got the time...
We've got the
INTIMATE MOMENTS

Passion. Suspense. Desire. Drama. Enter a world that's larger than life, where men and women overcome life's greatest odds for the ultimate prize: love. Nonstop excitement is closer than you think...in Silhouette Intimate Moments!

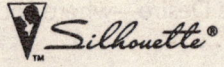

SIM-GEN

Silhouette ROMANCE™

What's a single dad to do when he needs a wife by next Thursday?

Who's a confirmed bachelor to call when he finds a baby on his doorstep?

How does a plain Jane in love with her gorgeous boss get him to notice her?

From classic love stories to romantic comedies to emotional heart tuggers, **Silhouette Romance** offers six irresistible novels every month by some of your favorite authors! Such as...beloved bestsellers **Diana Palmer, Annette Broadrick, Suzanne Carey, Elizabeth August** and **Marie Ferrarella**, to name just a few—and some sure to become favorites!

Fabulous Fathers...Bundles of Joy...Miniseries... Months of blushing brides and convenient weddings... Holiday celebrations... You'll find all this and much more in **Silhouette Romance**—always emotional, always enjoyable, always about love!

SR-GEN